A Demigod's Saga

T0078257

A DEMIGOD'S SAGA

THE BIRTH, THE BETRAYAL AND THE BEGINNING

DEEKSHA PUROHIT/
BHAVESH PUROHIT

PARTRIDGE
A Penguin Random House Company

To order additional copies of this book, contact
Partridge India
000 800 10062 62
www.partridgepublishing.com/india
orders.india@partridgepublishing.com

PREFACE

Our great ancestors and their successors have witnessed many wars during their time. Since ancient times, mankind has always been a threat more to himself than to others. The two epic battles of Mahabharata and Ramayana did not quench man's thirst for satisfaction. Though the two battles were glorified on the belief that they were fought against evil but one didn't realized at the end it was mankind that suffered the most. The nature of human beings for a worldwide authority could be easily felt even today. We are so desperate to make our lives better than our counter parts that we are even ready to take a stand against our own race. Mankind is bent upon to extinguish even its own kind. Without realizing the present and potential outcomes we are not interested in keeping quiet.

In the beginning of 20th century, the two World Wars proved too costly for us. The century marked the beginning of a tradition when one country became the enemy of another. Be it US vs. Soviet Union or India vs. Pakistan or there are multiple examples in the history books. But with the onset of 21st century, mankind faced another type of threat. Something which was never witnessed before; this time the threat was from inside. The several wars made us a witness to the loss of millions of our own race. We became wise and decided not to fight against each other. But, interestingly we pledged not to fight against each other's country and not against our own nation.

We now started to breed a new kind of war. This war includes various riots, Naxals attacks, terrorist attacks etc. They like saas-bahu daily soaps became a common part of our everyday existence. We became adapted to this threat and lived in an illusion, the illusion of being protected from these threats. But, in reality we feared from them the most.

The question which arises here is that who are these people who want to harm their own brothers and sisters? Is it just a sense of lust that is driving us to fight against each other or it something else? Whatever it maybe, the most important thing is that mankind is facing a serious threat, the threat that comes from mankind itself.

We portray a society where we stand together as brothers and sisters believing that "United we stand and Divided we fall" but unfortunately we are just portraying it.

Someone needs to step up. Some great people did it in the past and were glorified as Messiahs in various ideological books. But, who is a Messiah in present times? Who is here to make mankind understand to rise above its narrow and selfish thoughts and stop tearing each other apart?

Maybe, it's high time that someone up in the heaven realize this too and send someone who not only make us believe that there could be a possibility of existence of a peaceful world but also make us rise along with him to make that dream of peaceful world come true.

CHAPTER 1

A Paradise, A Jannat but most importantly it's the Heaven. Heaven as imagined by many is still a treat for the eyes in today's world scenario as well though some minor cracks could be easily seen but still it is at its best. There are not only huge and magnificent residential palaces rising from the heaven's waterbed but also the astounding landscape along with the honesty and trustworthiness of its citizens that add to the heaven's beauty.

In this heavenly kingdom, lives the creator of our universe, our Father. Our Father has always been a true witness to all the doings of mankind, be it when men learnt to produce a fire for its survival or be it when men took up weapons to fight against another man again for its survival. What is termed as the beautiful creation of our Father is with passage of time showing its ugly side. What hurts our Father is that his creation is fighting against each another for no such good cause. They are fighting just to fulfill their selfish needs.

Seeing his human dynasty reaching the peak of its degradation, our creator decides to find a solution before any calamity erases away even the traces of human existence. He summons up all his fellow wise Kings and Lords to discuss the problem mankind is facing and discover an appropriate solution to it.

All his wise men came running seeing the urgency with which their Father had called them. The wise men were not aware as to what was the reason behind such an urgent meeting. They gathered in a huge hall where the proceedings were to take place.

Soon, Father walked in and all the wise men stood up as a sign of respect towards their creator. Father accepting the honor, reaches his mighty throne and asks his fellow court man to begin the proceedings. The court man begins by saying, "We have gathered here for a special cause. Our Father seeks his wise men advice over an issue." The court man steps aside after declaring this. The hall is dead silent. Each wise man is thinking what could be the issue.

Lord Jal rises from his throne and asks," Dear Father, what is this all about? What is the issue that is making you so unrest?"

Father seeing his fellow wise men's anxiety replies," My fellow wise Kings and Lords, I created this universe and handed it over to you all to take care of my beautiful creation. But with time what I am witnessing is that my creation is approaching an end. I do not blame you, my wise men. The force responsible behind such a dramatic downfall is the mankind itself. What I demand from you is that I need a solution to stop mankind from hurting itself. It gives me great pain to see my creation blindfold destroying itself. So please, my dear wise men, you are requested to help me in this matter."

Once the Father had finished, the court starts whispering with each wise men discussing with one another the solution to the problem. Lord Agni as furious as a fire and without thinking much rises and says," Dear Father with all due respect, I see only an end to the mankind. What I propose is to re-evolve the mankind from the beginning again."

There is uproar in the hall among the wise men after hearing to Lord Agni's words. Father calms his wise men down. Finding an opportunity to speak, Lord Vayu says," Father, Lord Agni's proposal is not appropriate. I seek no end to mankind". Lord Agni getting furious replies," Lord Vayu, if you seek no end, then please guide us to avoid it." Lord Vayu replies," Lord Agni, I don't have any suggestion for the problem but I totally disagree with what you think."

Lord Jal interrupts the two wise men and says," Wise men, don't fight. Lord Agni, I also feel your proposal is completely out of context. Why not think over the problem with a cool mind?"

The three wise men get seated when Lord Thunder says," Father, I have a better alternative to the problem. There are multiple examples in history books where we visited earth and helped mankind in one form or the other; be it Lord Rama or Jesus Christ. People tend to follow the extra ordinary qualities of our avatar be it their sacrifice, their love, their affection. I, therefore, propose sending an avatar among the humans like we did in ancient times."

To this Lord Vayu says," Lord Thunder, your suggestion is good but you need to understand that this is not like the ancient times when we send our avatar among humans and get our job done. The thinking of humans has evolved. They will never going to believe in our avatar."

Suddenly, there is a spark in Father's eyes and he makes wise men listen," My dear wise men, I understand why we can't send our avatar or something like that among humans. Though the thinking of humans might have evolved to a great extent but I believe that they will always going to hear to the voice of their creator."

Listening this, there is even a bigger uproar. Lord Thunder says," But Father, I didn't mean to say that you should be going on earth to do this cleaning up work?"

Lord Jal says," Yes, Father. Lord Thunder is absolutely correct. I don't think this to be a solution. I do not support your idea of yourself going there among humans. What's your need to go out there?" Lord Agni continuing with the thought of his fellow wise man says," Father, your creation might be the best thing that ever happen to this universe but honestly speaking they don't deserve you. They are so stupid and foolish that they will not even care to listen to you."

Father replies by saying," But, someone needs to go out there." To this Lord Vayu replies," Then Father, let it be someone from among us but leaving you aside. We will not be able to see you in pain down there." This time all the wise men agree to Lord Vayu.

But Father does not want to lose one of his fellow wise men. So, he says," I have already suffered a lot of pain by seeing my children harming each other on earth. I will not be able to bear the same pain for anyone of you because you all are also my children and are very close to my heart. Do not ask me to do that."

Lord Agni re-iterates his proposal by saying," Father, we can't see you suffer among humans and neither can you see us suffer the same. Then, there is only one option left; the option of re-evolution of mankind."

Lord Thunder, lost in his thoughts, replies by saying," Father, wait a minute. Children; yes, Father; a child; a demi-god." The entire court is dead silent.

Father understanding the idea of Lord Thunder says," Fellow wise men, after listening to all these thoughts, I will just say someone will have to step up. We cannot wait a human to do that for us. You do not wish to send me down there and neither can I send you down there. I cannot re-evolve mankind for I still believe there are some noble souls left on earth and they should not suffer due to others. Therefore, I believe and support what Lord Thunder proposes in front of us. He wants a demi-god among humans. So, be it. I will be sending my own child among humans. He will be special from others because he will going to lead mankind in a direction that will help the humans stand tall and not stand divided."

Seeing his option losing ground, Lord Agni argues and puts his point by saying," Father, with due respect and honoring your judgment but by going with your solution, it could prove to be a real disaster."

Lord Thunder interrupts Lord Agni by saying," Lord Agni, just think before you say anything. How can you even doubt the thinking of our Father and question his judgment?"

Lord Agni says," First of all, demi-god was not our Father's solution to the problem but it was yours. So, I was questioning and doubting your thinking and not of our Father."

Lord Thunder loses his cool at once and replies," Lord Agni, mind your thoughts because they will mind your sayings."

Seeing a spark turning into a fire between the two wise men, Lord Vayu says," Lord Agni and Lord Thunder don't fight like humans. Use your wisdom. Lord Agni, I also think Lord Thunder is absolutely right about the solution. If you do not think it to be the right thing to do, then please let us know what is the reason behind such a thought?"

Lord Agni says," Dear Father, we all know what a child means to the parents. A parent always supports the child in every doing and guides the child throughout his life. What I fear is that if you will be sending your own son down there among the humans, then will you not be worried about his doings? Will you not try to guide him? Will you not try to help him? I do not say that don't help him at all but the thing is that it would be better to let him understand the mankind in his own terms and at the end of his life, we decide whether the judgment taken by us today to send a demi-god was worth a decision or not." The entire court supported Lord Agni but Lord Vayu and Lord Thunder could easily feel the ego that was hurt of Lord Agni by his spoken words. But for now, they could not understand what was going through Lord Agni's mind or what was he planning. So, they too decided to support him.

Father finally calms down the court room and says," Dear wise men, I understand your cause of worry. Therefore, I pledge my work will be just to give birth to my son and nothing else. I will never going to trace my son during his journey on earth and nor will I guide him. I will also let you decide as to who will be his earthly parents. I shall presume that whenever something good happens my son would have a hand in it and whenever some evil rises my son will fight against it till his last breath. I will only meet him when he finishes off the job for which he is being sent to earth. I promise to you all."

Getting the confirmation from Father, Lord Vayu asks Lord Agni," It's really a shame to ask our Father to pledge for something he is doing for a greater cause. But, still our Father loves and respects his wise men and therefore, condemns detaching himself from his son completely till his son meets the destination of his journey. Lord Agni, are you now satisfied or do you need anything else?"

Lord Agni says," Lord Vayu, don't get carried away in the flow of emotions. I did this for the sake of mankind. And in fact, my respect for our Father has increased several times after his brave decision. I am satisfied now. We, therefore, with approval of everyone can now definitely proceed towards the next big step."

Chapter 2

It was a normal summer afternoon and people were eagerly waiting for some monsoon showers to relieve them from scorching heat when suddenly everything changed so drastically that they could not react to what happened. From nowhere, clouds ran in and not even a single shadow was visible anywhere and there were apparent signs of thunder. But with the speed the thunder came, with the same speed it went away and lasted merely a minute. Many could not understand as to what happened for they were so busy in their lives that they couldn't react to what happened a minute ago. They were not even curious to know what caused such a dramatic climatic change. But the people who were free from their work and still couldn't react to the sudden climatic change also were not even curious to know rather they too left it for meteorological and news department do the work for them. In fact, the news departments too proved to be clueless.

That one minute, in which hundreds of people were not even able to react; that same one minute brought infinite source of happiness to a couple. The couple gave birth to a baby boy. It was their second child. No one gave attention to the signs or omens as this was the demi-god who has been sent on earth to give direction to the mankind in the years to come.

A god among humans was born. He received a thunderous welcome to earth. Who knows this may prove to be the happiest day of life not only for the couple but also for the child because of the most hardest part of their lives was yet to come. Neglecting all the worries, the couple was overjoyed for this was their 2nd child during their 10 years of marriage and they were delighted and graciously accepted this gift from their creator.

The couple named this young boy very aptly as Dev. Up in the heaven, Father was informed that his child has taken birth and also all possible links of communication between him and his son have been disconnected forever.

Dev's earthly parents, Anoop and Gayatri Narayan belonged to the middle class of society. His father is a local businessman who is a highly respected figure in his field while his mother is a house wife. He has a brother, Pallav who is a year older than him. His father though did have a lot of friends but among them his dearest one was Atul Kulkarni, a junior police inspector. Atul like Dev's father is an honest and respected figure in his department too. He was considered a family member by Dev's father and used to visit them regularly. He was among the first one to notice the extra talent which Dev boosted of.

Though Pallav was older than Dev but since birth it appeared as if Dev was older than his elder brother. Dev received the love and affection from every member of the family and the neighborhood. First, Pallav also appreciated his younger brother's out of earth like talent but with passage of time he started to envy Dev. Though younger than Pallav, Dev was fast able to overtake his elder brother in every field of life from academics to sports to extra-curricular activities. In every field he was better than his elder brother. Pallav tried his level best to grab attention from everyone and many times in trying to do so his every act became a piece of laughter in the house. He was just not able to understand as to how to get that elder brother position back from Dev. While on the other hand, Dev always respected his elder brother and even used to step back from certain competitions so that his brother could win it. But, Dev's every act was creating a dividing line between the two brothers. The harder Dev tried, the stronger the line became.

Pallav started to feel like a minor. He cannot live in the shadow of his younger brother. After some time, the two parents also started smelling the bitter relationship between the two brothers. They tried their level best to keep their family together but their efforts went in vain. Dev was not at fault; his extra ability cannot be termed as a mistake. On the other hand, Pallav was not ready to listen to his parents. Many a times, the couple hid the failures of Pallav and used to tell him in privacy rather than in front of Dev. This further fueled the tension between the two brothers. Even both the parents were tired of trying their level best.

One such day, when Pallav was in his higher secondary school, his father came to his school and took Pallav with him before the school could got over at its usual time. They went straight to a bakery where their family used to celebrate their weekends and also every small success in their lives. The bakery was an ordinary one but it was very famous all across the town. It was a blend of tradition with a little modernization. A lot of people use to gather there on weekends and on big occasions in their personal lives.

But, since it was a normal working day afternoon, therefore the entire bakery was almost deserted. The father-son duo took a window seat and following the usual routine, his father ordered some pastries and cake. After finishing the snacks, Pallav asked joyously his father," What's the matter, dad? What is the big occasion today?"

His father in a very subtle tone replies," Son, you have failed in the secondary school exams."

Pallav was heartbroken. He did give his best efforts during the exams. Before Pallav could speak anything, his father continue," Son, don't worry. We will start afresh. We will practice more because there is nothing that can replace practice and as you know it practice makes a man perfect."

Pallav says," Dad, we come here when we achieve something whether it maybe big or small in life. But dad, all this is a failure. Then, why did you bring me here?"

His father replies," Son, success and failure are the two faces of the same coin. Sometimes, we succeed and sometimes we fail. What's important is how we take our success and also our failure. I just wanted to let you know to treat failure and success in the same way. Failure is as good as a success if we are ready to learn something from them and especially from the former. And, when it comes to family and society, then let me tell you, son, you are closest to my heart. You will always find me, your mother and also your brother to help you at every step of your life. And, that's why just to make you realize the real essence of your life I brought you here."

Pallav suddenly realizing about his younger brother that he will have to study with him despite being elder than him, get agitated, stands up from his chair and angrily replies," Dad, I hate you. You didn't bring me here to make me realize that you all are with me but rather you wanted me to realize to cooperate with my younger brother and take help from him because now I will have to study with him. Dad, let me tell you, till date I only hated Dev but from now on you have also lost your respect in my eyes."

With these words, Pallav ran out of the bakery. His father tries to follow him till the gate of the bakery but couldn't match pace with his elder son beyond the exit point of the bakery.

CHAPTER 3

Dev's father returned home once again disappointed. He was about to enter the main gate when he notices his dear friend was already in the house waiting for his arrival. Atul was talking to his younger nephew, Dev.

On seeing Dev's father, Atul remarks by saying," Where are you now days? You appear a lot tired and frustrated."

Anoop handing a briefcase to Dev replies," Atul, I am busy uniting my family. Pallav is not able to digest the huge success his younger brother is achieving in every facet of life."

To this, Atul says," Hey Anoop! Don't think so much about that. These are everyday family issues. It is a story of every household now days."

Atul taking a brief pause says," Why don't we go somewhere? It's been quite a time since we went for a trip. Why not we all go to Nainital? It's a beautiful place and I have a house there right in between the mountain hills far away from the chores of the city. This trip may create wonders and you will be able to give quality time to Pallav also."

Signaling Dev to go inside and help his mother, Anoop says," Now, why do you require a break? Already, your job is tension free."

Atul replies," It's been not so easy now days. A new gangster, named Nawaz Sarraf has popped up from nowhere and he is really leading the local goons pretty well. It's almost impossible to catch him. Even if you catch his trained people, they will die but will not speak a word against their leader. I thought to go for a week break and it will help both of us to refuel our batteries. You will be able to spend some time with both of your sons and I will get some time to peacefully think over this new Nawaz Sarraf matter. So, what do you say?"

Anoop says," It's really so good to have a friend like you. But the thing is that if I can't reunite my family by giving them time over here then how can I do the same over there? And also, we are too busy in our lives. It would be impossible to even take a week off from our daily routine."

Atul says," I really thank God. If it's that hard to maintain a family, then I am happy being a bachelor all my life."

Anoop says," I knew you could never be a family man. By the way, just be careful of that Nawaz Sarraf."

Atul replies," Don't worry. No evil can run far away from the hands of law and jurisdiction. One day, we will catch him. Leave that gangster aside, what will you do now of Pallav? It appears he is really getting out of your hands."

To this, Anoop replies," I am trying my level best. And as you know time is the best healer. Maybe with passing of time, I do think that each and every thing will fall back into its proper place. Till then, just keeping up my spirit."

Atul says," You are a great man and a very good father as well. I really believe in you that one day you will sort out the matter by yourselves. I should leave now. It's too late in the night."

With this, Atul leaves for his house and Anoop also returns back to his family life.

CHAPTER 4

Days, months and years roll by. On one hand where Dev was about to complete his graduation while on the other Pallav joins his father's business. Anoop is now retired and looks after Pallav's work occasionally.

On one such day, Anoop finds some irregularities in Pallav's work. He discovers that he is rendering help to Nawaz Sarraf under the business that he started long time ago. He comes to know that all the accounts are fake and his business is in great loss rather than in profit as was falsely stated in the accounts.

Anoop gets fired up but finds himself in a dilemma. He cannot straight away talk to Pallav about this because when the last time father-son talked about the latter's failure, the discussion was not a pleasant one. When Anoop was thinking all about this, Dev suddenly calls him to have dinner.

Anoop goes straight to Dev and says," Dev, let's go for a walk."

But Gayatri insists to have dinner and then go for a walk. Dev's father agrees and they both enjoy their dinner together.

The father-son walks out of the house on to the main road. When they were all alone, Dev curiously asks his father," Dad, what's the matter?"

His father replies," Dev, I have always loved both of my sons dearly and have always tried to help you both.

Dev, you know Pallav is your elder brother but still he needs more guidance than you. You have an inborn gift and I really appreciate that. But, I am really worried about Pallav. I have a genuine feeling that he is in a wrong company. His accounts depict profit but rather we are in loss. Dev, by now you and I both know that you are here for a special reason. You have such extra-ordinary abilities that no human ever possessed. Dev, I need your word. I want you to promise me that despite being a younger brother you will always going to help Pallav. You will never leave him alone. Whatever he asks, you will going to provide him. Promise me, Dev."

Dev gets emotional and says," Dad, why are you talking like this?"

Anoop says," Dev, promise me. I don't know how long my stay on earth is. I want assurance that there will always be someone around Pallav to guide him, to help him."

Dev says," Don't talk like this, Dad."

His father insists," Dev, promise me."

Dev finally says," Dad, I promise you. I promise you that I will never lose Pallav at any stage of life. I will always help him whether that means even to give up my___"

Before Dev could say that, his father says," Dev, do not ever say that. Your promise is all I need and not your life. You have been an obedient son to us and I thank you for that."

Dev simply smiles and gives his father a warm hug. Suddenly, a high speed running truck ramps into the father-son standing on the footpath.

Chapter 5

Ironically, Dev's father dies on the spot while Dev escapes unhurt. To Dev's horror, he didn't got not even a single scar from the accident. Dev was over-flowing with agony, pain and revenge in his heart. He wanted to avenge his father's death.

Police and ambulance arrives at the accident spot. Police takes the truck driver into their custody and also takes Dev along with them as a witness of the accident.

At the police station, Dev's Uncle Atul Kulkarni meets him and consoles him of his father's death. Atul promises Dev that he will try his level best to punish the accused. But Dev wanted to take the revenge by himself.

He sees the accused walking out of the station and meeting his owner. Dev makes an excuse and goes straight where the accused went and waits at a distance for the accused to return back. Dev could not see the face of the owner as he was standing in the dark but when the truck driver was returning back, Dev lands a hard hit on his body and the driver goes flying into the police station's front wall. The impact was so hard that the entire wall crumbles and falls and the accused was declared dead on the spot.

Atul sees all this and before anyone could make what all has happened and also in order to protect Dev, Atul takes Dev away with him.

On the way, Dev's uncle stops his car at the gas station to refuel his vehicle. Dev was sitting hand-cuffed in the back seat. He was casually looking around when he sees a group of college students screaming and enjoying their time while refueling their vehicle at the same gas station. Dev was about to look somewhere else when he notices that one of the student who was having a half burnt cigarette in his hands casually throws it on the ground. First, Dev doesn't focuses on it but suddenly he realizes that wind is blowing that cigarette in the direction of gas reservoir. Dev sensing danger breaks his hand cuffs, slams the door open and runs out off the car straight to the reservoir. Atul sees this and warns Dev to stop running away. He feels that Dev is trying to run away. So, he pulls out his revolver and points at the running Dev. He warns Dev to stop but Dev was in a completely different world. He could only sense the approaching danger and nothing else. He was only focused on that cigarette and even when Atul starts firing at his legs, Dev do not stops and so, Atul is forced to fire at his chest. The bullet could not pierce even the skin of Dev and fell before it could have hit Dev's body. Before Atul could realize what Dev was doing; the cigarette had reached the gas reservoir and fell into it. As soon as cigarette fells into the reservoir, Dev too jumps into it. There is sudden eruption of fire all around and Atul is shocked and is completely immovable. But within a few seconds and before the erupting fire could have done some serious damage, it suddenly stops.

Moments later, Dev flies out of the reservoir completely naked but dipped in a thick layer of oil. He had soaked the entire heat energy produced by the combustion of fuel in the reservoir.

Atul at one end is shell shocked as to what happened while on the other is very pleased for he always knew Dev possessed something extra-ordinary. Dev lands himself in front of his uncle and suddenly goes unconscious. Atul holds Dev by his shoulders; grabs a blanket and puts around Dev's body to cover it.

He calls for emergency services and then takes Dev far away from the city.

CHAPTER 6

Dev was unconscious all the way. Dev's uncle after driving for some time parks the car in front of a deserted bar. After some time, Dev gains consciousness. He looks here and there but finds no one. He steps out of the car. It was early morning. He was gaining his ground when he saw his uncle coming through the gate of the bar. He was carrying a glass of water for Dev. Before, Dev could ask anything and Atul sensing his curiosity says," How are you, Dev? I was too worried about you after what all happened last night."

Dev replies," Uncle, what happened to me? I feel so weak."

Atul says," Nothing, you went unconscious." After drinking some water, Atul hands Dev some spare clothes from his car. After getting dressed, Dev and Atul both sit by the vehicle when the latter says," Dev, your father was not only a great man but also a dear friend to me. We shared each other's joy, sorrows, troubles, happiness, worries and everything. What happened to him last night cannot be undone."

Dev feeling guilty says," But uncle, I committed a murder yesterday. I really feel guilty."

To this Atul says," No, my son. You don't have to feel that way. The accused was found drunk at the accident spot. The law would have done the same what you did to him. So, don't worry about him. He was a criminal and he deserved that. Maybe, tomorrow he would get drunk again and repeat the same offence with someone else. That's my opinion and those who think you did wrong, then your heroics made up for your wrong doing" referring to Dev's life saving act at the gas station.

To this Dev says," Those were not some heroics. I just felt danger and so I acted."

Atul says," What so ever it was, your heroics or your act it was just fabulous. And Dev, life always gives us opportunity to mend our mistakes. Its' up to us whether we accept those opportunities or shut the door to those opportunities. If we accept them, we feel relieved and if we reject them, then we always try to run or hide from our mistakes. You might have made a mistake but you were courageous enough to mend it. By the way, I have informed your mother about your father's dismal. They want to see you at the earliest. I told them that you were a little disturbed over the whole accident, so I took you out with me."

Dev says," Then we should hurry back home."

Atul says," Wait Dev, there has been a thing about which I wanted to talk to you for a while. I want you to understand this. Dev what you did at the police station and at the gas station were 2 different things. One you did was for your own selfish fulfillment and the other for the sake of humanity. See, I have always believed in you. Your father always used to say to me that,' Atul, I have always praised this young lad but I fear that someday, he should not lose his path. He is a gifted child and I do not want him to get carried away by our pity emotions and do some wrong act. I want him to trust his capabilities and back it up to stand for humanity against all odds.' You have something in yourself which is beyond any human capabilities. Your father believed in you, I believe in you and now, I want you also to believe in what you really are. You run like anything, bullets can't even touch your skin, you defy gravity and you possess much more powers that no human can match. The thing is that it's up to you to decide whether to use all this, all this unlimited power for a greater cause or not. The path of selfish fulfillment will lead you to darkness whereas the path to help humanity will make you a legend. It's up to you to decide which path you want to travel. The latter one will test you; you might be asked to sacrifice your dear ones but maybe yours and their sacrifices will be worth of the trust they have it in you. So Dev, choose wisely."

Dev after giving a deep thought replies," Is there a way I choose the latter path and my dear ones do not get hurt due to it?"

Atul says," Well, of course, its' easy, put on a mask."

CHAPTER 7

The last 24 hours have been like a roller coaster ride for Dev. He witnessed his father's death, he murdered a criminal and then to amend his mistake he avoided a catastrophe to happen at the gas station.

On his way back, he sees a large crowd gathered in front of his house. He makes his way through the crowd and enters his house. He sees his mother weeping and sitting at one end and other women trying to console her. At the other side, he sees his brother talking to the neighborhood men, maybe telling them how and where the accident took place.

Pallav seeing his brother whispers," The person who should have died returns alive and the person who should have returned is no longer in between us."

Dev though got furious, but didn't wanted to create a scene in front of other people. He understood the need of the hour and the prevailing atmosphere. He tries to distract himself when he sees a known face standing at the far side of the house, draped in a traditional Indian dress, aptly fitting the cause for her presence. The young girl was Vidya.

Dev starts walking towards her. He recollects the fond memories of the time he shared with Vidya for these memories gave him a little distraction from the entire saddened atmosphere.

It all started when Vidya joined Dev in the higher secondary class. She was one of those prettiest girls to whom every boy was attracted to. Many tried but all failed. Even Vidya was also not a step back. She too spent her entire time roaming with her friends, bunking classes and lectures. And why would she be worried about her studies? She belonged to a wealthy and an influenced family. For her studies was fun. She knew that her wealth would get her admission in any college of her choice.

Vidya had a very strange outlook towards life. She believed in breaking 3 things in life—rules, bones and hearts. She believed that she could make anyone dance on her whims and wishes. Her magic made her the heartthrob of entire school but Dev was Dev. Vidya and Dev though were in the same class but never looked at each other leave alone engaging in a conversation. On one hand, Vidya thought Dev to be as boring as the books are while on the other she could never fit in the working of Dev. So they stayed away from each other.

Their egos collided with one another multiple times. Dev used to excel in every activity; be it dramatics, debating, sports or athletics. But, Vidya was as dumb as anything else. She was cool for no reason and Dev was best for everything you throw at him. And maybe that's why Dev too was a lot famous in the entire school among all the teachers and the students. Natasha was also one of them who appreciated Dev's abilities. She has been a friend to Dev from their primitive class in the school and used to feel always attracted towards the dynamic personality of Dev though she never told Dev about what all she felt for him.

Among all the boys who had a crush on Vidya also included Pallav. Since, Pallav failed in his secondary school exams, so he studied higher secondary school along with Dev and Vidya. Pallav, unlike any other guy was strongly attracted towards Vidya.

One day, Pallav was continuously staring Vidya when his best friend Gaurav says," Looking like this will not going to take this matter forward." Pallav says," Gaurav, I was thinking about taking a chance."

Gaurav says," What chance?"

Pallav doesn't say anything but Gaurav understands what Pallav meant. Gaurav says," You must be kidding me. If you are serious, then do it when she is all alone."

Before Gaurav could finish, Pallav stood up and started walking towards Vidya. He went straight to her and says," I want to be your boyfriend. Will you be my girlfriend?"

Vidya was sitting with her entire group of people around her. First, no one heard what Pallav said, so second time he shouted and said," Vidya, I love you." Now, this time not only Vidya heard it but also the other students who were sitting around Vidya. Vidya, a little surprised, says," Excuse me, but do I even know you?"

Pallav says," You must be joking, right? We are in the same class."

Vidya says," No, I am serious. Well guys, it's really a serious thing that I don't even recognize my classmates."

Pallav says," Well, whatever it maybe but Vidya I am serious about you."

Vidya says," You are serious about me for what?"

Pallav says," Vidya, I love you."

Vidya says," That's almost all of them do. So, should I accept everyone in my life?"

Pallav says," But, I am serious about us."

Vidya says," So, you love me?"

Pallav says," Yes, of course. I do."

Vidya says," Then you have to prove it."

Vidya's one of the friends, Nikhil interrupts and says," Hey Vidya! By the way, your new lover is the brother of our 'Mr. Perfect' Dev."

To this Vidya says," Oh ho!! Tell me you love me more than your brother?"

Pallav says," Yes, I do. And he is not my brother."

Vidya says," Ok, that's it, then. Prove your love to me by slapping your brother."

Pallav says," That's it. You have made my work even easier."

Dev was sitting at the far corner of the cafeteria with his friends including Natasha. He was completely unaware of what was and what will go to happen with him. Pallav along with Gaurav walks straight to Dev. On the way, Gaurav says," But Pallav, he is your brother. You cannot hurt him just for a girl."

Pallav says," Of course, I can. And also I told you, I do not take him as my brother."

Pallav reaches Dev. Dev was busy eating when Pallav says," Dev."

Dev stands up and says," Brother, what's the matter?"

Before Dev could even finish, Pallav lands a tight hit on Dev's face. The entire cafeteria falls dead silent. Dev was shocked but doesn't say a word. On the contrary, he just left. Pallav walked back to Vidya and says," Now what?"

Vidya was surprised how easily he slapped Dev and Dev didn't even responded. Vidya says," Good!! For now, your application is under process. We will let you know as soon as you get accepted."

Vidya was about to leave when Dev with a very stern face appears before her. Vidya feeling a sting of fear says," Hey man!! It was just a joke. Don't take it too seriously."

Dev smilingly says," I just want to say Thank You."

Everyone is surprised as to what Dev said. Dev turns around and was about to leave when Vidya says," You must be kidding me. You own me an explanation for this, in fact to all of us."

Dev stops, turns back and says," I am serious, thank you. By the way, you and your friends are too petty to understand this."

Vidya is too shocked to say anything but feeling a little insulted, she jokingly says," That means anyone will slap you and instead of replying back you will just say thank you. What a way to hide cowardice. Well then, I too would like to have that opportunity."

Vidya takes a step towards Dev to slap him but Dev holds her hand in mid way and stops her from hitting him.

Dev says," It's not an opportunity and I told you, you are still a milk feeding baby. You will not going to understand this."

Dev was not saying to insult someone but now Vidya's ego did got hurt. He left Vidya's hand. Nikhil steps in, pushes Dev a little bit and angrily say," Say sorry to her." The tension was building up and students start to gather around them in a circle in the cafeteria.

Dev says," I will not apologize to her. I was just trying to teach her some manners for I thought her father is too busy counting notes that he didn't teach her some."

This time Vidya completely lost her cool and says," Dev, it's too much. Either you apologize by your own will or they will make you say sorry forcefully."

Nikhil says to Dev," Dev, I am asking you last time; do what she asks from you to do."

Dev says," My answer is still no."

Nikhil says," Ok then, Dev. You left us with no option. It would be a little painful for you but I hope it ends soon."

Nikhil was about to hit Dev when Vidya steps in and says," Wait. Do not waste your energy. Let Pallav do this for us."

Dev realized that Vidya was using a brother against another brother. But, Dev too was determined not to hurt his brother. He felt that maybe after a couple of hits, Pallav may stop hitting him. But, Pallav was ruthless. He started landing punches after punches. Pallav used everything to anything to hit Dev; be it a tray, a chair or anything else. But, Dev didn't reply any of them.

Dev neither was ready to apologize nor was going to hurt his brother. So, he quietly took the beating. After some serious hits, Dev fall on the ground. Seeing Dev not even trying to protect himself even though he easily could have, suddenly Natasha comes in between Dev and Pallav and pleads to Vidya saying," Stop it, Vidya. You also know it is meaningless. Please, stop this."

Vidya was agitated by the sudden interruption in her entertainment and asks Nikhil to take Natasha away. Nikhil tries to move Natasha and when she opposes, Nikhil tries to hit her when Dev intervenes and with his full strength first blocks Nikhil from hitting Natasha and then lands a tight slap on his face and says," First, learn to respect women." Everyone was surprised at what Dev did. For once, a thought came in everyone's mind. If Dev had so much strength then why isn't he stopping his brother from hurting him? Dev moves Natasha out of the crowd, makes her sit on a chair and then comes back in the middle of all the live action and then to everyone's surprise, he again positions himself in front of Pallav to continue what the latter was doing. Sensing the situation getting out of control, Vidya says," Just stop it. That's enough."

But, Nikhil had other plans. He wanted to avenge the slap which he got from Dev and opposes Vidya and says," Continue beating. It's great fun. Let him get one thing straight; apologize or fall."

Vidya insists Pallav to stop. Pallav obediently stops but Nikhil pushes Pallav and says," Arc you a cattle? Just continue hit your brother."

To this Pallav says," Mind your tongue, Nikhil. I was doing this for Vidya and not for you."

Nikhil feeling insulted lands a tight slap on Pallav's face. Dev was now too much fired up. This time he backs himself and beats Nikhil and his fellow friends who tried to intervene very badly but he doesn't even touch Pallav not even once, leave alone beat him. Gaurav sensing no end to this forces Pallav to leave.

Vidya sees all this but didn't say a word. After beating Nikhil and his fellow friends, Dev turns to Vidya and says," Thank you." With this, Dev too leaves bleeding heavily.

Vidya was shocked so much that she couldn't even move a single step. She was feeling too low and had a hundred questions in her mind for Dev.

CHAPTER 8

It was in the afternoon when all this took place. The cafeteria authority filed a complaint in the principal's office against what all happened some minutes ago. Dev and Vidya were called in the principal's office turn by turn. Principal assured Dev of a strict disciplinary action against Vidya and her friends but Dev was too reluctant to file complaint against her.

Vidya was waiting outside the principal's office when Dev came out. He didn't say a word to her and just gave a smile to her and left. He was still bleeding a little bit. Vidya was continuously staring at him.

Vidya entered the office. Principal asks her to take a seat. Before she could say anything, the principal in a very serious tone says," Vidya, I know what all happened and who all were involved in that incident. I don't care who your father is. I believe in Dev and wanted to suspend you for what you did to him. But, unfortunately Dev didn't filed a complaint against you. So, you are free to go but mind it, anything like this will never be tolerated again."

Vidya was again surprised but thanked the principal and left the office. By now the school was over. Everyone was leaving their classroom when Vidya went back to her class to collect her bag. She was too lost in her thoughts that she was about to leave when she sees Dev's bag was also there in the class. She realized that Dev was still there in the school and had not left for his home. So, she came out to find Dev. While she was searching, she encountered Dev's friends. She asked them about Dev's whereabouts. They told her where they last saw Dev.

The moment she came to know where Dev was, she ran straight to find Dev. She didn't even bother herself to think where she was going. Her legs were just taking her to some desired location.

She reached where Dev was. She opened the door and went in. Dev was cleaning his bruises when he saw her but he preferred to stay quiet.

Vidya just stared at her. She went closer to Dev and helped him clean his wounds. Suddenly, she realized the reason for which she was here.

Vidya taking a step back says," Dev, I am sorry."

Dev doesn't reply back. Vidya continue saying," Dev, I know what all happened out there could have been prevented but I was too foolish to understand you. I just wanted to make you feel low and myself superior to you. I am really sorry for that."

Dev gives a glare at her but still doesn't say a word. Trying to ease a strange atmosphere, Vidya says," I am Vidya, student of St. Xavier's; presently in high school. Will you be friend of mine?"

Vidya stretches her hand for friendship but Dev was still not interested in talking or even replying to her.

Vidya feeling a little tense says," Dev, I am trying so hard but you are as adamant as nothing else in this world. You should have at least appreciated me for my courage and determination for coming and meeting you in a boy's fresh room."

Yes, there was she. That day, Vidya was too low that she could have done anything and went anywhere in order to apologize to Dev.

This time finally Dev says," After what all happened, you were supposed to."

Vidya says," What is the problem you have with me? You reply to everyone like this only or is it just with me?"

Dev once again goes silent. Vidya continues," I mean the way you reply to me as if you don't want to talk to me."

Dev says," You got it right."

Vidya a little surprised says," What so ever, you keep your rude attitude with you. I was just here to sorry and thank you both. I am sorry because you got hurt just because of me and thank you for not complaining it to the principal."

Dev says," I told you already you need not apologize for what happened out there. Rather, you did a favor to me and I returned it back to you in the principal's office."

Vidya says," By the way, why didn't you complaint against me to the principal?"

Dev was finished doing his cleaning of his wounds when he says," Let's move outside. It's not an appropriate place to talk and also if someone sees us together over here, it will create a whole new problem for no good reason."

Vidya realizes and they both leave the room before anyone could spot them there. They pick their bags from their class and starts walking towards the main gate of the school.

Once out, Vidya says," You owe me an answer."

Dev says," Oh yes; I forgot. First of all, I told you I wanted to return your favor. And secondly, what good it could have done to me if you were suspended from the school. Had your father come to know, he would have given you a tough scolding for that. And this way, you would have learnt nothing and would dare again to do this with some other guy at some other place. And also had I complaint; who knows you would have again set me up for a tough beating?"

Vidya says," No, no, definitely not since we are now friends."

Dev says," When did we became friends? I didn't accept your proposal."

Vidya says," You didn't but neither did you decline it."

Dev says," Smart thinking. I appreciate that."

Vidya says," So, we are friends now?"

Dev jokingly says," Your application is under process. We will let you know as soon as you get accepted."

Vidya realizing that she said the same to Pallav in the cafeteria, they both break into laughter when Dev says," Ok, you and your friendship proposal is accepted."

They both reach the main gate. With this, their little conversation was over but a new bond had definitely been formed. Somewhere down the line, Vidya was feeling a change in her. Whatsoever it may be, they both say goodbye to one another and heads away to their respective destination.

Pallav arrived much before Dev came back home from his school. As usual their mother was there at home to welcome both her sons. Since, Pallav arrived first so she saw his swollen hands. She asked him what happened but Pallav made an excuse and said he was forced to lift a heavy thing.

But when Dev came back and she saw his bruised up face, she eventually realized what must have happened with their sons back at school. She asked Dev too and Dev also tried to make an excuse but she caught him.

His mother said," Dev, I saw Pallav's hands. I know what must have happened but I just wish to know that you both are safe and sound."

Dev says," Yes, mom. We both are alright."

His mother says," Dev, such acts may provoke more anger in him."

Dev says," Mom, I just want him to accept me as his brother. I will do anything to get that done."

His mother says," Dev, it's good that you are standing by your brother and you are having such a strong belief in him but Dev I want you to be cautious about one thing."

Dev says," What is it mother?"

His mother says," Dev, just make sure you support him only when he is right; do not ever support him when he is wrong rather scold him for his wrong doings. Today, it might be he is right but Dev I don't think so that it may last long. Going by the prevailing condition of his life, one day you will have to take a stand against your brother too."

Dev says," Mother, that's what I am trying to avoid."

His mother says," Dev, I really appreciate your efforts and my blessings are with you that you will succeed in avoiding any such day when you will be forced to stand against your very own brother."

To this Dev says," I am trying my level best but if such day comes then I will treat him as my opponent in the battle and not by brother."

His mother says," As a mother, I too do not want to see that day ever come in my life. But Dev, if that day comes then you already know whose side I will be on."

Dev says," Mom, just leave it for that day. For now, I am hungry and I am dying to have some food. So, please can we have some food to eat?"

CHAPTER 9

It all changed after that. Vidya stopped roaming with her hopeless friends. She started to company Dev and used to spend most of the time along with Dev and his friends. She became sincere in her studies too. She realized that maybe what all happened that day was not at all good but it definitely changed her for good.

Dev too started to enjoy his life spending time with Vidya. They used to study together, eat their lunch together. Though Dev used to be with Vidya for most of his time but he never opened up with her too. Vidya used to feel like Dev was hiding something and she was correct too as Dev had secrets.

Once Vidya was sitting in front of Dev in the library while he was preparing his presentation. Suddenly, Vidya started talking. She says," Dev, do you have a girlfriend?"

Without thinking for a moment, Dev replied back," Yes, I have one."

Vidya a little shocked, curiously asks him," You never told me, who is she?"

Dev says," Don't worry; you are not the fortunate one."

Vidya was a little depressed when Dev realized it. So, he says," You will not ask me for my boyfriends?"

Vidya again a little shocked," What!! I thought till date that you were all right."

Dev says," Yeah, I know!! It can happen with anyone."

Vidya angrily asks Dev," Tell me the name of those 2 idiots; I will get their thinking straight."

Dev says," I don't think so you would like to beat my father like the way you once forced my brother to beat me."

Vidya says," What!! I don't understand."

Dev, with a smile replies back," I was just kidding. My 2 boyfriends are my father and my brother and accordingly, my mother is my one and only girlfriend."

Vidya takes a sigh of relief. She pinches Dev hard and says," Why do you play such serious pranks."

Dev says," By the way, what was so serious about them? Can't I have a girlfriend and a boyfriend?"

Vidya says," You don't seem appropriate to have a boyfriend and about the girlfriend issue I will take care of that."

Dev says," Please explain."

Vidya jokingly says," Since, you have 2 boyfriends and only 1 girlfriend, so it doesn't seems balanced up. So, what I was thinking, to balance the variables on both the sides."

Dev says," But, how can you even think of removing my father or my brother."

Vidya says," Intelligent Dhakkan!! You must be kidding me. I mean to say let's add another girlfriend to your life so that it gets balanced."

The bell rang and library time was over. Dev says," I know."

Vidya getting a little shy says," If you know it, then say it, Dev."

Dev jokingly says," I know that you will find me a suitable girlfriend because I don't think till date I ever met a girl who can be my girlfriend."

Vidya angrily says," You know Dev, you are such a jerk. Here is a girl who wants to be your girlfriend and on the contrary you want me itself to find you someone else."

Dev smilingly says," Hey, I was just joking."

Dev was about to leave when Vidya says," So . . . ."

Dev says," Ok, it can work fine with me."

With this, Vidya was over flowing with happiness. At last, it's official. They both left the library together.

CHAPTER 10

Time passed by. Dev, Vidya and all their classmates cleared their final exams and moved to the last year of their high school. This time in the final exams to everyone's surprise Vidya gave a tough fight to Dev for the top spot but was still forced to satisfy with the second spot.

One day after the school got over, Vidya and Dev were walking back together to the main gate when Vidya says," My dad is so happy with me. He has never been so delighted with my progress in my entire school life. There have always been complaints about me but since the past 8 months or so there has been a terrific turn around in everything. Complaints have turned into praises, my academics have improved and I have been able to win a couple of runner up trophies all thanks to you since you have been the winner in every competition. It's all because of you. Thank you, Dev."

Dev accepting the gratitude says," Give a little credit to you as well. I just did what it would have needed to get you back on the right track. And also, always try to win by defeating the best; either be the best or try to become the best by defeating the best in the business."

Vidya says," But, still it's all because of you. By the way, my dad asked me about such a sudden transformation. So, I could just say one name, Dev. It's all because of Dev that all this happened and he got so much impressed by your praises that he told me to call you home at any convenient day."

Dev feeling a little shy says," Vidya, thanks for the praises. But, right now I am too occupied with Pallav. He is just losing control on himself."

Vidya says," I never understood what's there in between you and Pallav. You call him your brother, you give him ample respect and in return he doesn't even accept you as his brother."

Dev says," I believe in him and one day he will realize that too. The thing is that I can never leave Pallav alone. He is my brother whether he accepts that or not. You remember I said thank you that day after you forced Pallav to beat me?"

Vidya says," Who can forget that? I was too surprised to see how ruthlessly he was beating you and you like a true brother didn't even try to stop him once."

Dev says," I wanted him to take out all the frustration and agony he had for me from a long time. You gave him the opportunity that day even though it meant to tolerate his beating. And, that's why I thanked you for giving me and my brother such an opportunity."

Vidya says," You are an epitome to your name, Dev. It's this selfless quality of yours that I love the most. Maybe, some day Pallav realizes your sacrifice."

Dev says," I can just hope that day come soon."

They now had to go their separate ways. But before departing, Vidya says to Dev," Dev, try and find some time to meet my father some day, please."

Dev with a smile on his face nods his neck in approval. They both depart finally to their separate ways.

CHAPTER 11

Years passed by. Dev and Vidya completed their high school. Dev joined a prestigious college of their city for higher studies and following Dev's footmarks, Vidya too joined him in the same college. She by now had become a constant companion to Dev; just like a shadow. She wanted to spend maximum time with Dev.

In the past three years, Vidya insisted Dev to meet her father several times but every time Dev had an excuse. Maybe, Dev didn't want to meet her father but he couldn't say so to Vidya for he feared hurting her. Dev somewhere feared that maybe Vidya's father not accept him although Vidya used to always praise his level of excellence in front of her father.

On one hand where Dev continued to study while on the other Pallav left his studies after his high school and joined his father's business. Pallav was constantly degrading his life; always running into trouble. He even joined hands with Nawaz Sarraf though no one in the family knew about it. Pallav used to provide aid in the free movement of Nawaz Sarraf's goods in and out of the city. In return, Sarraf gave him security against the local goons. He was doing all this under the name of his father's business, so no one ever suspected it until one day while going through his son's work when his father noticed the unusual accounts and their detailing.

He wanted to talk about this to his son but rather went to Dev and was about to talk to him when the accident took place.

By now, Dev reached Vidya. Vidya tried to console him by saying," Hey Dev. It was really sad to hear what happened to your father."

Dev simply nods and then he says," Can we go for a walk?"

Vidya says," Dev, your mother needs you now the most though Pallav doesn't."

Dev says," Yeah, I know. But there are already too many relatives to support her and Pallav is there too to support her. I just can't see all this weeping and crying. It just suffocates me."

Vidya says," I would have preferred you to stay here with your family but if you insist let's go for a walk."

They both leave from the back door towards the main market. It was early morning so there was no chaos on the streets. The streets were deserted.

They both were walking silently when Vidya tried to break the silence and say," So, your equation is once again unbalanced now."

Dev was deep in his thinking and therefore was not able to catch in one attempt what Vidya said. So, Vidya repeated what she had said moments before to Dev.

Dev was unable to understand it. So, he asks her," I don't get it."

Vidya says," Arey, I am talking about your 2 boyfriends and 2 girlfriends' equation. Now, since you are left with 1 boyfriend and 2 girlfriends, so, I have a fantastic offer for you."

Dev says," What, now you also want to leave?"

Vidya says," Sadu, you can't think the other way round. I am saying marry me. Now, this will have 2 advantages. First, my father will then become your father-in-law and this way you will once again have 2 boyfriends."

Dev says," And, what's the second benefit?"

Vidya says," Hmm, you can get a huge share of my father's business in the form of dowry."

Finally, Vidya gets a smile on Dev's face. Dev says," If I had loved you for your money then by now you would have come to know about it."

Vidya says," I was just joking. By the way, why don't you marry me? You and I are both eligible now to get married."

Dev says," Why are you in such a hurry to get married!! Let me enjoy my bachelorhood."

Vidya says," Oh ho!! Bachelorhood!!"

Dev says," Just kidding."

Vidya says," So, you too have started to play jokes now days."

Dev says," An effect of companionship."

Vidya says," Good going, boss. By the way, you can at least meet my father?"

Dev says," I am looking forward to that sooner or later."

Vidya says," Let it be sooner and not later."

Dev nods in approval and they start their return journey back to Dev's house.

CHAPTER 12

Following his father's dismal, Dev took the advice of his uncle seriously and decided to fight away the local mafia and bring peace to his city. He decides to design a costume but he was not able to give a name to his costume when he consulted his uncle.

His uncle says," Well, it's too easy. I have always believed that you are our creator's special child but on earth you also have human parents too. So, there is one famous word which we use in our Hindi language, Yaksh. It means a demi-god; an angel who has one parent up in the heaven and one on earth. I think it will aptly suit you."

Dev says," Uncle, thank you. I am really grateful that you are always there to guide me."

Uncle says," Dev, it's my pleasure to guide a person like you and never forget I am always there for you."

Dev says," Thanks a lot, uncle. And also, just keep your police force off me."

His uncle says," Don't worry; they will not going to harm you."

His uncle says," So, when are you starting?"

Before his uncle could even finish his question, Dev hung up the phone. Maybe, it all has to start now. A journey that will going to test Dev like never ever before.

CHAPTER 13

A black costume with a logo depicting Yaksh written in front in dark blue and red shades was a new life of Dev. Dev promised himself that he will never let his family come to know about his dual life and this also included Vidya too. It will be a secret kept between him and his uncle; that's it and no one else will ever be told about this; for this may compromise his family's safety.

Dev took off his new life on a holiday late in the day. He as promised to his uncle kicked off by taking up local goons. He raided a small consignment deep in the narrow streets where the mafia thrived.

The local goons were not able to understand as to what was happening to their fellow mates. Yaksh took them one by one and beat them up very badly. Police feared the narrow streets so much that they never dared to enter those streets but today was a completely different day. Yaksh led them straight into the heart of the thriving mafia's business empire. Yaksh tied every local goon somewhere or at the other place in the streets; some to the electricity poles; some were even fitted into the walls. By the time, police arrived, Yaksh had done his job.

That day if Nawaz Sarraf too would have been there, he too would have landed straight into the bars. Yaksh didn't know about Sarraf's absence rather he attacked the mafia thinking to take down Sarraf in one straight go. He later came to know that Sarraf operated somewhere from outside the city while interrogating one of the criminals.

The next day newspaper flooded with the news of Yaksh. The local people who took photographs of Yaksh in action gave them to the newspaper agencies while getting some income in return.

Yaksh, Yaksh and Yaksh; everywhere from newspapers to news channels; even general public didn't stopped talking about him. He became an overnight hero. People became eager and curious about their new hero and wanted to know the maximum about him. But, their every try was in vain.

Yaksh could never be found out anywhere else except where crime thrived. It gave a courageous boost to the police forces even though first they opposed Yaksh but later realized that somewhere he did gave them a push or an opportunity to curb the crime in the city.

Yaksh continued his work. Every now and then, the mafia was going down heavily. No one was able to even raise voice against Yaksh. He drove away the mafia and their crime far from the city in a month time.

Now, people lived freely; free from fear of criminal activities. They now had the freedom to live their lives on their own terms and conditions.

Dev's uncle kept his promise and assured his police department that Yaksh was on their side. They need not hunt Yaksh rather stand with him to take down the mafia.

The rigorous efforts of Yaksh saw mafia stepping back; either they surrendered or ran away. The power and strength of Yaksh sent shivers of fear in their spines. Now, only Nawaz Sarraf was left. But, unfortunately he could not be found. Yaksh tried his level best; used his uncle's resources but to no advantage. Nawaz Sarraf was untraceable.

CHAPTER 14

On one hand, Dev was busy with Yaksh while on the other his family recovered from the sudden demise of his father. Pallav continued with his father's business but now things changed.

With Yaksh removing the influence of Nawaz Sarraf completely from the crime that was thriving in the city, it also removed the aid that Pallav used to get against the local businessman. Now, the local businessman started demanding their money which Pallav had lost in their combined business.

Pallav faced more troubles now since he was no longer needed by Nawaz Sarraf anymore because of Yaksh's acts. Yaksh blocked the free flow of Nawaz Sarraf's goods in and out of the city; now not even Pallav could do anything about this.

Pallav was now left with nothing to do as his main business was brought to a standstill by Yaksh. But, he hid this from Dev. And Dev was too busy with Yaksh that he was not able to concentrate on Pallav. Earlier, his father used to keep a watch on Pallav's actions but now there was no one left to stop him from harming himself.

The local businessman whose money Pallav lost in their combined business during his early days started harassing him to get their money back. They started hiring local goons to scare him. One day late in the evening, in the market when Pallav was returning from his usual business work, the local goons tried to beat him. They attacked him when he was leaving his office. Though the goons were told only to scare Pallav a little bit but seeing the audacity of Pallav, they become too irritated and try to force Pallav to death. Pallav somehow manages to steal a bike and tried to run away from them. The local goons were not ready to let him go so easily, so they too decide to chase him and close his chapter forever. Seeing this, Pallav accelerates his bike and start driving rashly when suddenly he gets hit by a black luxury car. The hit was too hard since Pallav was riding his bike at a great speed. The owner of the car was himself driving the vehicle and when he realized that he had hit someone, he parks his car in a corner and quickly jumps out of the car. He was an old man; not so old but still was in mid 50s or 60s.

He saw Pallav on the road bleeding very badly. So, he immediately called the emergency services. By the time, he called for emergency services, a large crowd gathers around the accident spot. Fearing the crowd's response and sensing Pallav nearing his death, the goons run away from the accident spot. Ambulance and police rushes to the accident spot.

Dev was at his home when his uncle calls him. He picks up the phone when his uncle says," Just leave whatever you are doing. Your brother has been hit. It's a major hit and he is bleeding very badly. We are taking him to the hospital. Try to reach there at the earliest. He may need your little help."

Dev was shocked but understanding the need of the hour summons his strength and makes an excuse to his mother. He feels it correct not to inform his mother of Pallav's accident.

He rushes rather flies; this time without his Yaksh costume straight to the hospital where Pallav was admitted. When he reaches there, his uncle takes him straight to the doctor who has been supervising his brother's operation. Before Dev could say anything, the doctor says," You are his real brother?"

Dev nods in approval when the doctor continues," See, your brother has gone through a serious accident and on the way to the hospital he had lost several units of blood. Since, it's an emergency we will not be able to arrange such a huge amount of blood. So,"

Before the doctor could finish his sentence, Dev says," Take my blood but just give me my brother back like the way he was prior to the accident."

The doctor says," I know that but the problem is that when I came to know that the patient has a brother that means you, I told him all about this."

Dev says," I do not understand."

The doctor says," When the patient was told that you are donating your blood to save his life he simply said that he will die but will not take a single drop of your blood."

Dev was too surprised listening to the doctor's words about Pallav's behavior but he knew what he has to do now. He asked the doctor the permission to talk to his brother for a minute. The doctor agreed but he also made it clear to Dev that they should operate Pallav soon.

Dev speedily moves to the cell where Pallav was lying. He was a little unconscious but was able to recognize Dev. Dev insists his brother," Brother, let me allow doing this for you."

Pallav reiterates his words and says," Didn't the doctor told you that I would rather die but will not accept your blood."

To this Dev says," Brother, don't be adamant. I know you hate me. But brother, this is for you. Please accept it and I will return that favor to you. I promise I will do whatever you ask me to do even I will leave your life forever if you ask me to do so."

Pallav sensing an opportunity agrees to Dev's wish but he too demands a favor in return. He whispers that in Dev's ears. Dev comes out of the cell and tells the doctor that his brother has agreed. The doctor quickly moves his brother to the operation theater. Dev donates his blood but all the time his mind was somewhere else. He was just thinking how to return the favor his brother has asked from him. Is it right or wrong to do what Pallav has asked him to do? Keeping all these logical questions aside he rather left himself flow with his emotions. For the first time, Pallav has asked something from him and he too promised his father he will give Pallav whatever and whenever he will demand anything from him and therefore he decides to do what his brother has asked from him.

After donating his blood, Dev comes out of the ward. He feels a little weak but realizes that there is some work that he has to do. While walking through the hallway, he calls his uncle. His uncle went to the station to file a complaint against the owner of the car that hit Pallav.

His uncle picked up the phone and before he could ask anything, Dev asks him," Tell me the name and address of the owner of the car."

His uncle without thinking much tells him," His name is Mr. Anupam Bansal. His residence is somewhere in posh region in the city but when I talked to him last he was in his office at 22, Malabar Coast."

His uncle became a little suspicious and before he could ask any further questions from Dev, Dev hung up his phone.

CHAPTER 15

Dev was feeling too weak physically after donating his blood but was rather too strong in his mind with his intentions. He took a cab for his destination. It took him almost an hour to reach where he was told to go by his brother to return the favor—22, Malabar Coast.

The one hour ride gave Dev some time to regain his control over his body and now he was feeling perfect physically. He asked the cab driver to stop 2 buildings before his destination point. Cab driver did what he was asked to do and Dev gets down. He soon saw the building where Mr. Anupam Bansal had his office. He went straight to the reception.

An old lady was seated at the reception when Dev asks her," Ma'am, I have to talk to Mr. Bansal urgently. Can you get me an appointment?"

The lady answered," Son, you can't meet him without an appointment and also he is about to leave for his house. It's too late in the day already. Please come tomorrow."

Dev knew he would not be allowed to meet the man but he wanted to confirm whether Mr. Bansal was still in his office or not. While returning he saw the exact location of Mr. Bansal's office written on the notice board. It was the 19th floor.

Dev came outside and went to the opposite side of Mr. Bansal's main office. It was pitch dark and no one could have seen him. So, he flew straight to the 19th floor.

He broke the wall and entered the building at the 19th floor. Security alarms went on and the entire building was locked down. Security guards rushed in to ensure safety of the staff members. The electricity was cut and only the emergency lights were on. The emergency lights were dim but still the path to Mr. Bansal's office was visible. There were not many people around; in fact the corridor was empty. Dev walks straight to Mr. Bansal's office. He was about to knock on the door but realizes the door was already open.

He enters the room without fearing that the old man can see him. Dev greets the old man but he doesn't receive a response. Dev does what his brother has asked him to do and then he flies back towards the hospital. This time too he lands himself much before the hospital in a dark area so that no one can see him flying around.

From there on, Dev starts a walk back to the hospital. This small walk gave him time to cool himself down and bring down his sentiments and control his over flowing emotions.

When he reached back hospital, he went straight to the ward where his brother was shifted after Pallav's operation was successfully completed. On the way, the doctors told Dev that his brother is out of danger but it will take him time to recover from his injuries.

Dev was over joyous by the news of operation being successful and forgot what he did some moments ago. Dev wanted to see his brother. He also decides to call his mother once he feels that his brother is out of danger.

He reaches Pallav's ward, grabs the knob and was about to open it when suddenly his phone rings up.

CHAPTER 16

It was Vidya who was calling. Dev first tries to ignore it but she calls him again. Dev releases the knob of the gate from his hand and turns around to pick up the phone. Dev says," Vidya, I am busy right now; will talk to you later."

Before Dev could hang up his phone, Vidya in a very heavy voice says," Dev." Dev realizes Vidya was crying and indeed she was.

Dev reacts back and says," Vidya, what's happening? And why are you crying?"

Vidya says," Dev, Dev . . ."

Dev says," Vidya, just say something. What's going on?"

Vidya says," Dev, I want you here."

Dev says," Just tell me what happened?"

Gathering some strength, Vidya says," Dev, my father is dead."

Dev says," What? But, how?"

Vidya says," He has been murdered."

Dev gets a little anxious and says," Vidya, where are you right now?"

Vidya responds by saying," I am at the accident spot. My father was murdered at his office."

Dev getting furious says," Vidya, tell me the exact location where the accident took place."

Vidya says," Why are you getting fired up at me? Note down the location; it's—22, Malabar Coast."

Dev realized something has gone terribly wrong. Getting no reply from Dev, Vidya says," Dev, you are coming?"

Dev says," Vidya, what's your complete name?"

Vidya getting a little irritated says," Dev, have you gone mad? My father has been murdered and you are interested in asking my surname."

Dev was now completely fired up. He says," Vidya, just answer me what I have asked from you."

Vidya says," Its Vidya Bansal."

Before Vidya could finish, Dev says," Vidya Bansal, daughter of Anupam Bansal; right? The same Mr. Anupam Bansal whose office is on the 19th floor at 22, Malabar Coast."

Vidya says," Dev, I am not getting anything. How do you know all this about my father?"

Dev could not say anything more. He realized what he has done. Vidya says," Talk to me, Dev. What's wrong?"

Dev had completely broken down. He answers," Vidya, listen to me carefully. Your father has been murdered."

Vidya says," Dev, I know it and that's why I want you to be here to support me."

Dev says," Let me complete, Vidya."

Vidya felt silent on the other side when Dev says," Vidya, your father has been murdered and I am the murderer."

Vidya was too shocked to answer. First she thought Dev must be joking, so she says," Dev, it's not the right time for your stupid jokes. Just get down here."

Dev says," Vidya, I am not joking. I am the murderer of your father. I came at his office some 2 hours ago and then threw him out of his 19th floor office window."

Before hanging her phone, Vidya says," Just get lost, Dev. You are beyond my understanding. I don't know whether you are serious or you are joking for no reason but one thing is sure I hate you and I don't want to see your face again in my life. Just get lost from my life."

Now, Dev too was crying heavily. It was a stark reality now that he unknowingly has murdered Vidya's father. The favor which Pallav asked him was to severely punish the culprit who hit his brother and Dev got carried away with his emotions so much that he murdered the old man who he now came to know was Vidya's father.

Dev's phone again rings up. This time it was his uncle. He picked it up and his uncle says," Dev, where are you? I know it's not the right time to disturb you but Dev; but there have been some serious trouble going on in the city. Dev, I just want to know that you do not have a hand in it."

Dev not knowing what to say but after giving a very deep thought says," Uncle, I have created a monster. Today, it's just impossible to stop me. You know the answer to the question you asked; just trust your instincts."

His uncle says," Dev, if it's true what I am thinking then son you have crossed the line today and also if it means that you will going to hurt my people then I will do anything to stop you."

Dev says," Uncle, I don't want to hurt you. Just leave me alone."

His uncle says," Dev, you have to pay for your wrong doing and today you will going to get hurt. Wait for me. I am coming for you."

With this, his uncle hung up his phone and asked all the city's police forces to head straight towards the hospital where Dev was presently there. Dev knew he needs to get out of there before his uncle come hunting for him.

While Dev was walking out of the hospital, he realized that his end is near. Vidya do not want to see his face again; his brother hates him and is handicapped and the person who gave him a reason to trust his extraordinary abilities is coming to take him down. Dev got too emotional and wanted to run away but before doing that he wanted to do one last thing.

Dev flies straight back to his home. He enters the house secretly but his mother notices it. His mother asks him," Dev, what is going on and where is Pallav?"

Dev says," Mother, everything is alright. Pallav met an accident but he is now out of danger. He is at the hospital. I have to go now, mother."

His mother says," But Dev, it's already too late. When will you return back?"

Dev says," Mother, trust me, I will be back when it's the most appropriate time for me to return." His mother was just staring at him but Dev could speak no more. Dev makes his mother unconscious and lays her on the bed. He quickly writes something on a paper and leaves.

Dev dons up his costume and goes straight to his destination. On the other hand, his uncle reached the hospital but was unable to find him. He issues an on sight shoot order for Yaksh and also alarms the entire police force to take him down wherever they see him.

CHAPTER 17

It was getting too late in the night. Police forces had by now covered every possible street of the city. The choppers had also been called in and every news channel was continuously flashing the news of the wide scale hunt that was taking place.

Dev's uncle made a news appearance and announced," I issue an arrest warrant against Yaksh and also if required to shoot him down too. Today is the darkest hour we ever witnessed in our lives because our hero has shown his true colors. He has been issued an arrest warrant in relation to the sudden trouble taking place in the city." Dev realizes after feeling the ruthlessness with which his uncle had issued an on sight shoot order against him that now it's all against him but he too was determined to do his last task.

Dev reaches his destination but on the way he gets spotted by a police chopper and the news spreads like a fire among all the police forces. They all come rushing in to take down Yaksh. By the time, they all arrived at the scene; Yaksh had already injured several security personal and had damaged the main vault of the bank too.

For everyone's surprise, their hero was robbing a bank in front of them. But, still they were not ready to believe it. They wanted to see it with their own eyes. They decide to wait outside heavily equipped with weapons for Yaksh to step out of the bank. Yaksh steps out of the bank carrying a few money bags on his shoulder. He sees that he has been surrounded by police forces from all sides even they have covered the aerial route as well. The spotlight was focused on Yaksh. All the police men had now pointed their guns straight towards Yaksh. Yaksh looked everywhere to find a place to escape but there wasn't any. While looking everywhere, he saw his uncle but neither of the two said anything to each other. They just gave a glare when his uncle announced on the megaphone," Yaksh, surrender yourself or else we will have to take you down. There is no way out."

This last saying added further fuel to Yaksh's anger and he decides to make his move. He looks here and there and then suddenly, he threw the bags straight high up in the air and made a powerful jump onto the opposite building. The police forces were left with no option but to open fire at him. But, Dev was too quick for them. The moment he made a jump into the opposite building's wall, the very next moment he makes another jump high into the air to collect the bags which he threw in the air. He lands on another building after collecting the bags. He was now out of sight from the policemen on the ground but choppers start firing at him. Yaksh very quickly chokes out a plan and decides to run through the streets rather on the top of the buildings. He then start running on the streets with a speed that it became almost impossible for the police forces to match pace with him. Even, the choppers were finding it difficult to continue tracing him as he was running fast and deep into the streets.

Yaksh started to draw all the police forces out of the city. When he reaches the far end of the city he then suddenly stops. He thought that he had lost them but the police forces were too determined to take him down. They chased him down till the far end and this time didn't even give him a warning and started the open fire again. Even the choppers were raining bullets at him.

Yaksh was now left with no option. He earlier thought that he could make an escape without hurting anyone but now he have to do it what he never thought of doing. He tied the money bags to his waist and then decides to take down the choppers first. He according to his plan straight away attacks the chopper. He swung the first chopper hard but before doing that he threw every crew member out of it. He swung it hard and targeting the second chopper he threw the first chopper straight at it. Sensing danger, the second chopper's flight crew too jumped off it before their chopper crashed.

The two choppers blasted and crashed on the ground. Yaksh was still in the air but by now the police forces have stopped firing at him. Maybe, they too realized that it was worthless. Yaksh turned and was about to leave when suddenly a bullet pierced his right leg and he tumbled midway in the air. He balanced himself and was shocked at the bullet piercing his skin for the first time. But he was fired up more and now wanted to take a full strength hit at the police forces. But, as soon as he turned to see who shot him, he was taken aback. It was his uncle who was still pointing a gun at him. Yaksh decided to leave now. His right leg was bleeding but he tried his level best to fly back. He crashed through the top of various buildings but finally reached his home.

Since, he drew all the police force out of the city, he had now purchased some time to clean up his wounds and change his costume too. He deposits all the money right beside the bed where his mother was sleeping and silently walks out of the house.

CHAPTER 18

It was almost dawn. Yaksh was gone now and Dev's uncle knew where Yaksh was headed to but still he ordered the police forces to start patrolling the streets trying to find any evidence that can lead them to Yaksh. Atul takes a vehicle with him and heads straight to Dev's house. He silently enters the house and sees blood spots all over the ground. He makes his weapon ready but soon realizes that Dev was no longer there.

He was about to leave when Dev's mother came out and says," The person you are looking for is no longer here. The money bags are there in my room. They do not belong here; just take them away."

Atul could not say anything but his mother continued and says," He left this here."

And she hands him a paper.

CHAPTER 19

Dear Mother,

It will be hard for you to believe that I too have fallen but sometimes even the best too fail. I have messed up many things in my life. I have committed such mistakes that it's hard to believe that I could ever be forgiven or not. I have hit the lowest in my life.

I know when everyone gives away, there is always a place called home which always accept you above your failures; there is a family. I found one and I am really grateful. I do believe in my family and I always know that no matter what may happen my family will never lose faith in me.

I have guilt deep down in my heart. I don't know whether it could heel someday or not. I am forced to leave it on time. Who knows, in my case too time may prove to be the best heeler. I want to leave now but as I promised you I will be back one day.

Mom, I have left some money for you and Pallav. I know you will be angry when you will come to know from where that money came but I wanted to be assured that you do not suffer because of me.

Today I came to know one thing I can never face in my life; it's my failures and my mistakes. I know you have and you will always going to support and love me but please forgive me if you can.

I hope Pallav recovers soon.

I assure you one day we will be back together as one big family.

Dev.

After going through the letter, Atul asks Dev's mother," I know it's hard time for you but if you have any idea where Dev has gone, please tell me."

Dev's mother says," If I had known, I would have myself gone and brought him back."

With this, Atul hands over the letter to Dev's mother and takes away the money bags with him. When he was about to leave, Atul says," If you need any help, just let me know."

Dev's mother says," I will. Atul, do you still believe in him?"

Atul says," When did I stop believing in him? I was just trying to slow him down because when he gets carried away, he doesn't care what is right and what is wrong. I wanted to prevent him doing the wrong thing. That's it and he was just not able to get this simple thing straight in his head. I am just disappointed that he did not listen to the right person. I promise you I will do anything to bring him back."

And with this, Atul too leaves.

CHAPTER 20

Once again newspapers flooded with the news of Yaksh but this time they were not praising his heroics. Photos, articles, police statements whatever and everything the journalists found was there in the papers. They only made impact on the thinking of the people and took away the title of savior, hero from Yaksh. Police was still searching for Yaksh but Atul was more interested in looking for Dev. But, every attempt was in vain.

It's too hard to find a person who himself doesn't want to be seen. Few days later, the arrest warrant changed into search warrant; further there was also a reward imposed on Yaksh. Police tried their level hard to find him but when there was no trace that could be found out, they too eased their efforts. Newspapers for some days continued publishing reports of the wrong acts of Yaksh but soon they too realized that it was worthless.

One day, the municipal committee along with senior officials of police department arranged a press conference and made a public statement stating," Despite continuous efforts of our entire police department, we have failed to find trace that could lead to Yaksh. Therefore, we have decided to move on and leave Yaksh behind. The arrest warrant will prevail and so the reward scheme."

The very next day newspapers flooded with the news of Yaksh going missing. Soon, people too forgot about their hero. They were back to their normal life. They were living in a belief that whatever Yaksh did prior to his robbing a bank will stay on forever.

The fear which Yaksh implanted in the minds of criminals was easily fading away with each passing day. Police though tried to resist them but once it was confirmed that Yaksh had gone missing; the police force also became weak and crime returned back to its normal life.

On one hand, where a new city was returning back to its older way of life while on the other Pallav recovered from his injuries way too fast. He soon got discharged from the hospital and came back to his old house to live with his mother. His mother told him that Dev had left. Pallav also realized that the favor he asked from Dev proved too heavy a burden on his brother's shoulders. And maybe that's why he left.

Soon, Pallav also realized the extra strength in his body. He used to think that as to how he recovered so early. He was rather feeling good about the accident for 2 reasons. First, his body was feeling too good now instead of feeling damaged and broken up and secondly, the person he hated the most, Dev was no more with his family and left.

Pallav joined back his business and once again got an offer from Nawaz Sarraf to rejoin hands. But, Pallav who was once betrayed by Nawaz Sarraf was no longer interested in once again doing business with Sarraf. He straight away rejected the offer of Sarraf's men and when they tried to thrash him, they themselves got a very bad beating.

He started feeling that strength in his body with which he could take down anyone. He also came to know about Yaksh going rogue. Realizing his true potential, he decides to step up and live a life of a hero.

He recreated Yaksh's costume but this time according to his body dimensions and decided to lock horns with the local mafia. He too decides to restart the legacy which Dev's Yaksh has left behind.

He made his first public appearance as Yaksh when he starts off a chase against the local goons in the night. The news of appearance of Yaksh after a month's interval time once again spreads like a fire in the whole city. The police department was in a dilemma whether to chase down the criminals or to take Yaksh down. But, they all decide that they can take these local goons down on any other ordinary day but Yaksh is the big fish now. Even, Dev's uncle was also interested in taking Yaksh down for he too believed that maybe Dev has returned.

Yaksh was chasing the criminals and he himself was being chased by the police. First, he thought that maybe police was trying to cover him up against the criminals. The three of them were following each other across each and every street as they continued chasing each other. Soon, Yaksh was about to catch the criminals when police decides to open fire at Yaksh. He was surprised as to what was happening. First, again he thought that maybe police were firing at the criminals and since he was in the middle of the two he was also facing the bullets. But, he soon felt that the police was chasing him down and not the criminals when police announced on the megaphone at Yaksh to stop running and surrender himself to the police.

Yaksh got furious and stopped chasing the criminals. He turned and now he was facing the entire city's police department. Yaksh stopped and so did the police department at a distance from him. The police official once again announced on the megaphone to force Yaksh to surrender but Yaksh was not interested in surrendering himself. He decides that he will not make the first move but rather allow the police to make a move.

Seeing Yaksh not moving at all, the police department decides to fire at his leg. They call Atul Kulkarni to take a shot because he was the only one whose bullet pierced Yaksh's body the last time. Atul took his gun out and aimed at his target. He fires the bullet.

As supposed, the bullet raced pointing straight at Yaksh's left leg and when it was about to hit Yaksh, suddenly it stops. Indeed, Yaksh had himself stopped it with his bare hands. He catches the bullet and sends it back rolling on the ground towards Atul giving him another chance to shoot the same bullet.

Everyone was shocked and frozen to the ground. Their best option to take down Yaksh had failed. Yaksh was now too fired up; he decides to leave and turns around. Seeing his back, police decides to open fire. But, once again Yaksh proved too powerful and he stops each and every bullet in air itself before the bullets could hit him and when the police officials stop firing to reload their guns Yaksh fires back every single bullet back at the police officers.

Several police officers got hit and were severely injured. Yaksh flew back as the entire scene became a blood spot. No one understood what was happening to their hero. They wanted him to surrender but rather he back fired at them. Dev's uncle Atul was one of the few who did not get shot. He took his vehicle and raced back to Dev's residence.

He reached there and angrily enters the house blasting away the doors. Pallav had already reached prior to his uncle and had changed his costume. He runs out to see who was storming in their house like that. He sees his uncle and politely asks him," Uncle, what's the matter?"

Pallav's mother too runs out to see what's happening. Atul says," You also know what has been happening. You didn't tell me that Dev is back?"

Pallav's mother looks at Pallav and says," Is he saying the truth?"

Pallav says," No, mother. I don't know about Dev and his whereabouts. I haven't heard of him since the day he left us."

Atul was a little surprised. He didn't know what to say. He just cannot ask his family about Yaksh because he promised to Dev that never Dev's family should come to know about his double life. So, he apologized and left.

CHAPTER 21

On the way back to his station, he was trying to figure out who actually Yaksh is. Upon reaching the police station, Atul heads straight to his private cabin and took out certain files to go deep into the matter. He tries to get all his facts together. He first thought that maybe this might be someone else because the bullet didn't even touch his skin but then he realized even Dev too was also powerful enough to stop that bullet from harming him. But, then who was the person behind Yaksh when he was shot in his leg before Dev left.

Everything was perplexing. Atul was too confused to understand anything. He decides to wait for some time before drawing any conclusions. He thinks that maybe next time when Yaksh appears again, he could gather some clues that might allow him to solve this perplexing puzzle of multiple Yaksh's.

But, Yaksh was gone. Pallav after reaching back home decides to take a deep thought about Yaksh. He thinks deeply in his mind," People hate Yaksh as if he is the villain of their lives. Police try to kill him as if he is the most wanted criminal of the city. Everyone wants him down."

Pallav thinks more deeply and realizes," If police and the general public want to hate me then why I do it being a hero? Why not turn myself into a villain and who said to change myself into a villain; I am already a villain. I was never supposed to do this hero thing. And with these powers by my side, I can rule over this city."

He decides to change. Not himself but the name and logo of the costume and therefore only the name and the logo were changed. Yaksh was now to be called Aksh. Pallav kept the costume same because he wanted to get the real feel while destroying everything good that Yaksh had created.

But, the big problem had surfaced now. Aksh was all over the news. Whether it was robbing or helping local goons, Aksh did every wrong thing to make himself the villain of the city. Police by now had become so weak and fragile that they pretended as if there was no Aksh.

Pallav as Aksh was good to a limited extent but Pallav wanted to rule his city as Pallav itself and not by wearing a mask. So, he chokes out a plan. Pallav takes some time out and goes and meets his school time friend Gaurav. He decides to make this short trip all by himself. Gaurav too was a complete broke and used to do small household works to keep his livelihood moving.

Pallav was already there at Gaurav's small house residence when the latter arrived. Seeing his best friend, Gaurav was too delighted. They both sat around a small wooden table and started to enjoy each other's company and recollected their past memories. Suddenly, Pallav changes the topic and says," Gaurav, I am not here for all this. I am here with a purpose. I want you to join hands with me and we can take down this entire city and rule it."

Gaurav says," Pallav, are you kidding me? There is this Nawaz Sarraf and now there is this new one too, Aksh. Who will even dare to raise their voice against them?"

Pallav says," Gaurav, I have a plan. The plan will make Sarraf kneel in front of us and don't bother about Aksh, he is on our side."

Gaurav says," Then, what do you need?"

Pallav says," I need a person who I can trust and presently I can only trust you. In return, I will provide you with something very special to me."

Gaurav thinks for a moment and says," Pallav, I am fine with my life over here. At least, I am assured that I will not lose my life."

Hearing Gaurav refusing his proposal, Pallav gets a little furious, smacks the small wooden table into the walls, moves closer to Gaurav and holds him high in the air by his neck and says," I don't think so now you feel like you are assured of your life? I guarantee no one will ever be able to touch you leave alone harm you. Come with me."

Gaurav grasping for air, says," Pallav, okay."

Pallav puts him down and says," So, I believe you are in?"

Gaurav takes a sigh of relief and then says," Yeah, what good is this life to me? Let's take a chance with you."

With this, Gaurav and Pallav shake hands and decide to start a new journey together.

Chapter 22

Pallav once realizing that everything is going according to his plans decides to take Nawaz Sarraf down. He gives a call to the men working under him about his intentions and announces," Stand by me because I stand by someone special. That someone special will fight for me till his last breathe. And that special one is . . ." Pallav looks to his left when Aksh steps in. Everyone gets a morale boost seeing Aksh on their side.

Pallav along with his troops marches towards Nawaz Sarraf's men. Pallav's men were less in number but they had a special weapon with them. On reaching the decided spot, Pallav asks his men to stay in their vehicles as he and Aksh steps out of the car to go and pay a visit to Sarraf.

For the first time Sarraf came to the town in the last decade or so. Pallav sat in front of Sarraf and Aksh was standing by him when Sarraf says," I heard about your work a lot."

Pallav replies back," It's good that you only heard and not saw it because if you had seen it then you would have not been alive today."

Sarraf's confidence took a hit by Pallav's reply but he was impressed too. He came straight to the point," Pallav, we both are lions and we are meant to rule. Then, why fight and make our own loses both in terms of time and money."

Pallav says," Correction needed; as you can see, you are no longer a lion now, you were a lion. Now, I am the lion and you are thinking to have a share of a lion's meat. It's quite petty of you."

Sensing insult, Sarraf's two of his strongest men try to approach Pallav to attack him when Aksh intervenes and using his full strength holds the two men by their neck and jams them into the room's walls. Sarraf was so shaken that he stands up from his chair. He was about to call more men when Pallav directs Aksh to hold Sarraf by his neck against the wall. Pallav moves closer to Sarraf and says," Moments earlier you said about mutual loss but I think it will be your loss only if you dare fight me. You see I have Aksh who can take thousand of your men down single handedly. So, I am giving you an offer. I will take control of the entire mafia of this city but under your name. You are going to make me your right hand and if you reject or oppose it then I will be forced to pull out your right hand permanently out of your body."

Pallav takes a pause and orders Aksh to ease the pressure on Sarraf's neck. Pallav continues," So, we have a deal, right?"

Sarraf was left with no option but to agree. He was feeling the heat of insult but he stayed quiet for the moment.

As Sarraf was leaving, Pallav tried to add further fuel to the fire by saying," Sarraf, send me the keys of your mansion in the city. You see a ruler like me needs to look and live like a ruler."

Sarraf looks at Pallav angrily but he can't do anything to him. He was forced to again nod in approval.

Days later, Pallav received the keys of the mansion and shifted his family and his business to the large bungalow.

His mother was too surprised by such a sudden change. She was curious to know about all this. Pallav simply said," A new partner was interested in our business. So, he made investments and we were able to get rich dividends in return."

While Pallav did all his black business under his father's name, it was not longer a secret that he was fully supported by Sarraf and Aksh. Police didn't even try daring a voice against him because he had everyone in his pocket.

The conditions and circumstances of the city were going out of everyone's hands. Crime was at its peak thriving at full capacity in the city like never ever seen before. Pallav's influence was so strong on everyone that soon he no longer needed the services of Aksh regularly. Aksh was still loyal to Pallav but reduced his frequent visits to Pallav's business meetings.

On one hand where Pallav was gaining momentum while on the other Atul tried his level best to find Dev. He too realized that Dev was not behind the mask of Aksh because Dev would never cross the limit to such a great extent.

Atul could never tolerate the crime thriving at full capacity in his city. But, he too was helpless. The top officials were a puppet in the hands of Pallav. It all came down to his police department but they too were also feeling the heat.

Several years passed by but there were no signs of Dev. Everything went on as normal as it could. People adjusted to the new conditions. They were left to believe only in their own strength. Even if public or some journalists tried raising their voice, they too were brutally punished for opposing the injustice that was taking place throughout the city.

Atul was too exhausted looking for Dev. He too realized that Dev was their best chance in taking a stand against the crime. But, he was completely out of reach of everyone.

The years strolled by but nothing changed. It was as if that the entire system had been crushed by a big heavy bulldozer. No one dared standing against them. By now, Sarraf, Pallav and Aksh had taken the crime to a brand new level never seen before. Though Sarraf was never happy with Pallav but he too was forced to work under him. Pallav was thriving like anything else and Sarraf was getting more and more impatient. He has always been waiting for an opportunity to strike Pallav but was till day, not able to find one.

CHAPTER 23

It's been 7 long years of wait but still there was no sign of Dev or Yaksh. Atul was getting more and more desperate to find Dev but there was nothing that could lead him to Dev.

Atul was like everybody else; about to lose hope of finding Dev. One day after getting exhausted of a complete day's work he came back home. After eating his food, he went and sat on the terrace and was still wondering where Dev could be. He was fired up with the thought that how could Dev not even leave a single trace behind him. He can't be that arrogant.

The thought of Dev might be dead by now was cropping up in Atul's mind but he always strayed these thoughts away. He could never believe that Dev could ever be dead. But, with time passing by and with no signs of Dev he too was not able to keep these wild thoughts away from him. Even, Dev's mother was getting sick and wanted to see Dev. Pallav now also wanted to find his brother for 2 reasons. Firstly, he wanted Dev for his mother and secondly, now he didn't worried about his brother's stature. Pallav himself was too successful that Dev would too have been easily over shadowed by Pallav's empowering business. Pallav one day met Atul privately and told him about his mother falling sick and her willingness to see Dev. Atul told him," Pallav, It's almost impossible to find Dev. He has left no trace behind."

Pallav says," Uncle, there is nothing impossible if you have the will and determination. I want you to find him at any cost. If you need any help in any manner, just let me know once. But, just find him even it means to bring from hell."

Atul says," I am trying my level best and Dev can't be in hell. He never deserves that place."

Pallav says," I don't want to see your efforts but what I want to see are the results of your efforts; what you have done so far are only efforts. I want to see them converting into results."

Atul says," See Pallav, if you are so desperate then why don't you ask your more powerful friend to help find Dev?"

Pallav says," I believe in you, that's why I am here. The day that trust is no more I will ask my more powerful friend to help me. I give you two months time; find me Dev or else you will be no longer needed."

In a way Pallav had given his uncle an ultimatum. Before leaving, Pallav says," And uncle, how can you even say that Dev deserved hell or not when you don't even have the slightest of the idea of what all Dev did?"

His uncle says," I have always known what I have to."

And with this, Pallav leaves him all alone. The deadline was too near; only a couple of weeks were left. Atul was still wondering where to go to find Dev. Maybe, Pallav was right about Dev being in hell. But, who knows.

Atul was all alone and was dearly missing his best friend, Dev's father, Anoop. He used to always say to Atul," Get married; have a family."

But, Atul too always used to ignore his sincere advice. Now, he was really feeling the loneliness but still he did had something to remove this loneliness too; his pleasant memories of his dear friend. He decided to give a little rest to his mind by reliving those fond memories again.

Atul was recalling the memories when he dozes off. He started dreaming of the memories when he recalls one in which he says to his friend," You are so tired. Let's go for a trip."

His friend replies back," But, where to?"

Atul answers," I have a house right in between the scenic mountains of Nai . . ."

He was about to complete his sentence in his dreams when suddenly rain started to fell and he woke up. He collected his belongings and went in. He goes to his bed and was about to doze off when suddenly he recalls what he dreamt last. He feels that something is wrong with his dream. He recalls that Dev was present and then very next moment Anoop signals Dev to go inside for some reason but the main point is that by then he had already told Dev's father the location of the trip.

Atul jumps out of his bed realizing a high probability of finally finding the exact location of Dev. He calls Pallav and asks him to send some strong men to him. Pallav was half asleep and was not in any mood to ask his uncle the reason. He thought that maybe his uncle has found Dev but realizing that all his uncle's efforts till now have gone in vain, he didn't seem interested in himself going with him and therefore decides to send a dozen strong men to his uncle's house and once again he falls back to sleep.

CHAPTER 24

"Dev, do me a favor if you wish to save my life."

"What? Just get lost from my life. I don't want to see you nor talk to you ever in my life."

"Yaksh, surrender yourself or else we will be forced to open fire."

No matter how far you run away but you can never run away from your guilt. It's been seven long years but that guilt is still there. It's been seven years since Dev left his family and moved here, living alone in a cottage deep into the forests surrounded by mountains on all four sides. Dev when came here first thought that maybe this scenic beauty will help him overcome his guilt but it was never supposed to be. Dev tried hard but never succeeded.

Sometimes Dev even thought whether it would had been better had he stayed back and faced the outcomes of his wrong deeds rather than running away from them. But every time he used to brush aside this thought. But, till how long?

The inner guilt always chases the culprit in one form or the other. In Dev's case, his guilt chased him through his dreams rather wild dreams. These dreams used to keep his wounds afresh. Every 2 out of 3 days he used to have these dreams and what follows next, gives him some work for the rest of the day.

It was another such dream where Dev recollects his last moments in his city. He is broken out of his sleep when once again he is unable to control his flowing energy and as a result he blows away the entire house in front of his bed. He soon realizes what he has done with his uncontrolled power. He decides to get to work so that he can finish it off before early dawn.

He gets off his bed, drinks some water, washes his face and heads straight to garage room where he keeps all his tools. While going towards it, he suspects that something is wrong. A forest never sleeps and this typical silence in a forest definitely indicates that something is going on. This could only mean that someone forcefully has made this forest sleep.

Before, Dev could turn and see through a window; bullets start to pierce his house from all sides. He falls to ground and crawls to a corner in the kitchen. After 2 rounds of firing, it suddenly stops. He realizes this as his window of opportunity to counter attack. Dev through a hole sees a dozen men fully masked standing with heavy weapons waiting for further instructions. Then, he sees two men start walking towards the house. They enter the house through the front door and then the other six also follow them to cover them up. Dev crawls and steps out of the back door.

He decides first to take the men down on the outside and then he will take the men inside the house. So, he attacks them from the back. He first beats every single of the firing crew which was standing outside. He speedily moves towards the front door of the house to take the rest of the men down too.

The eight people who had entered his house had broken themselves in the teams of 2 each and started searching for their target. Before, they could realize that they had lost their four supporting people; Dev already entered the house without getting noticed.

Dev starts taking each of the team down. The firing crew realizes that they are under attack but they just can't see their target. With every passing minute, one of the members was going down. They panicked and decided to gather in the dining room. When they gathered, they realize that only four of them were left. Sensing danger and threat, they start firing in all the possible directions. Dev hid himself by sticking to the roof and when they stopped firing to reload their guns, Dev attacked the remaining four as well. He beat each one of them heavily before they could even react to Dev's swiftness. He left one to have a personal interview with him.

Dev angrily asks him," Who sent you here?" The last person was so scared that he doesn't answers back. Dev thinking him to be useless take him down too. But before Dev could turn around and leave, a gun was pointed at his head. Before the man pointing the gun could say anything, Dev says," Be a man. You should have attacked from the front and not from the back."

The man replies," When you can hurt my men from the back then why can't I do the same to you too?"

The man continues," You look better doing these things in a costume rather than in these clothes."

Dev says," At last, there is someone who can talk."

To this the man replies," Why? I thought you were enjoying your loneliness."

Dev says," By the way, if you know me so well, then you should also know that these bullets do not harm me."

The man replies back," Don't be so confident. I was told that when you were seen last in the city, a cop fired and his bullet for the first time in your entire life pierced through your skin. Didn't it?"

Dev says," Well, there are some exceptions."

The man says," These exceptions could prove to be too harmful for you and by the way who said I want to harm you?"

Dev was a little shocked. So, he asks," Still so much affection for me after what all I did? And if you do not want to hurt me, then why are you here and who are you?"

The man replies," Son, I want you back. Your people need their hero back. By the way, I am the same person who gave you the address of this place."

Dev easily understood who the man is. The man lowers the gun and Dev turns around. The man removes his mask and Dev says," Oh God! This, I must be dreaming."

CHAPTER 25

The man was his uncle, Atul himself.

After all the high adrenaline action was over, there was only that kitchen which had suffered the least damage. So, Dev offers a chair to his uncle and he himself grabs one too. Dev's uncle takes the seat offered and sits down while Dev fetches some water for his uncle.

While Dev was fetching water, his uncle asks him," How are you, Dev?"

Dev says," I am doing well. But, what about you?"

Atul says," Yeah, I too am fine. By the way, what is this new look about? Let me tell you if you kept this look to hide yourself from your acquaintances, then you are wrong because you are still the same except this dirty looking long beard."

Dev says," You got it wrong. I was forced to keep it because it's hard to find a barber in this area. So, I try doing it by myself once in 5-6 months."

Atul says," So, I presume you must have learnt a lot in hair cutting by now?"

Dev simply nods and serves a glass of water to his uncle. Atul says," Thanks for the water."

He continues," That's good. As you didn't complete your graduation, therefore when we return back you will need some job to fill your empty stomach. Right, Dev?"

Dev says," Wait, wait . . . . Who are we here and I am better off as being someone else rather than a barber."

Atul says," As you can see, I am taking my remaining left over house back and since you would be homeless so I prefer you return back to your previous old home."

Dev says," No, no. This is not happening again."

Atul says," Yes, it is. You are coming with me and so is Yaksh along with you."

Dev says," Ok, now I get it. This is all about Yaksh. What is your plan now? Once again make me the good guy and then throw me out. Force me to stay away from my family for such a long period of time again? I will not allow you to do that again. You are here to take Yaksh back and not me. Do you know what it is called, Selfishness?"

Atul says," Dev, calm down. First of all Dev, you ran away because you chose it that way to hide your mistakes. You were never thrown out of our lives but the thing is that what you did on that day was a big mistake after all. And whether it had been someone else, he too would have been forced to account for his mistakes. It was up to you to decide whether to stay back or run away and you chose the latter one."

Dev says," So, according to you I chose to run away. But, if I had stayed back that day you would had shot me down. Have you forgotten or I have to remind you again that you tried to shoot me and unfortunately you succeeded in doing so too."

Atul says," I never forced you to run away. That day, I wanted you to slow down. Do you know why Dev?"

Dev says," Continue. I want to hear it."

Atul says," Dev, you were too focused in your job that you were running behind everything. What it did to you was that you stopped thinking what is right and what is wrong. You were just rushing through your work and that's what the origin of your mistakes to follow was. Had you stopped for a second and thought logically whether what you were doing was right or wrong, I assure you, you would have got the answer. On that day, I was just trying to help you by forcing you to slow down."

His uncle takes a break and then continues," Dev, you look calm today. Maybe, that's what this wait of seven long years has given it to you and you are still focused even today. You know what you have to do but you have a fear somewhere in your mind or in your heart. You are trying to hide that fear by blaming your mistakes on others. Dev, don't do that. Give voice to your fear and I promise you I will help you to overcome it."

CHAPTER 26

After taking a deep breath, Dev says," I fear facing my mistakes and failures. It's not that I have never done it before facing all these but this time it's different. Even such a long wait of seven years has also not able to make me forget my mistakes. Still, they haunt me in my dreams."

To this, Atul says," Dev, the real essence of life is not in how many times we fail but how many times we rise above our failures. We all commit mistakes; some knowingly and some unknowingly but the thing is that some dare to convert these mistakes into a window of opportunity to prove themselves right again and some hide away thinking one day time will heal everything. Dev, sometimes it's up to us whether to take a stand for our wrong doings or leave it on time. In your case, you yourself will have to make everyone believe in you again."

Dev says," But, how? They all hate me."

Atul says," You said about time heeling up our mistakes but let me tell you what time does is that it changes our feelings towards each other. The people who did hate you 7 years ago now they themselves want you back. Dev, your mother too wants her son back. She is dying, Dev. Even the luxuries provided to her by Pallav are also not able to cure her. Maybe, you are her cure. She wants to see you back. And if not for her, get back for your brother. He is ruthlessly engaged in harming himself as well as the entire city with the help of his powerful friends. Dev, do what you are best at. Make sure people start trusting you again."

Dev says," The situation looks pretty grim though. Uncle what if I return back but still people do not accept me?"

Atul says," Dev, why are you thinking so much? Just get back there and do your job."

Dev says," I have to think all this because people expect something from me and what if I again fail to deliver?"

Atul says," People have expectations from their heroes, role models and you are one of them. But sometimes they too fail to deliver but it doesn't mean to run and hide away from them. These mistakes; these failures makes us realize that we too are humans. We try; sometimes we succeed and sometimes we fail. It's all normal, Dev. The thing is that when we fail, do we have the courage and strength to fight and stand back?"

His uncle takes a pause and says," Dev, I had, I am and I will always going to see that courage and strength in your eyes; in your personality that can make you rise above your failures."

Finally Dev says," You will never going to lose hope on me?"

Atul says," How can I lose hope on someone who is my very last hope?"

Dev simply smiles and stands up to give a warm hug to his uncle and says," But uncle, tell me one thing. Why do you need Yaksh back so desperately? I almost finished off the crime before I left and there was no one left behind."

Atul says," There was no one only for the first few months and the moment the mafia realized that Yaksh is gone and soon it opened floodgates for them to flourish."

Dev says," So, who is it now? Who is so powerful enough that you were not able to stop him?"

Atul says," Actually, it all started because we were not sure about Yaksh."

Dev says," What are you saying? I left a letter behind with my mother which clearly stated that I have left."

Atul says," Yes, I know. But the thing is that some weeks later of your departure, Yaksh was reported to be seen in the streets. First, I didn't believe it but when I myself saw him, I was just shocked like nothing else. We chased him but we ourselves got a beating from him. Days later, the news came from inside that your brother will now be leading local mafia. Again we were shocked because your brother was not powerful enough to suppress Sarraf and lead by himself but when we came to know that he was supported by a much powerful friend of his whose powers and strength had no match, we became confident that something was wrong. We started to find more and more information regarding your brother's powerful aide. Do you know what we came up with?"

Dev says," Yaksh."

Atul says," Nope, it was now Aksh. Yaksh who was last seen when we chased him down had now changed himself into Aksh. More bad news for us."

Dev surprisingly says," What?"

Atul says," Yes, Yaksh is now called as Aksh and has a hand in every wrong thing happening in the city."

Dev asks," But, where did my brother find him?"

Atul says," Till date, we don't know about that. But the thing is that, from the day they both joined hands, everyone has become a puppet in their hands."

There is a pin drop silence before Dev says," So, now I have to once again dress myself as Yaksh and fight that Aksh?"

Atul says," The thing is that Aksh looks completely similar to you except the logo. So, in a way you will have to redesign your costume again."

Dev says," That's rude of him."

Atul says," Dev, I want to make you realize beforehand itself that Aksh is too powerful. Don't take him too lightly."

Dev says," I have never taken my opponents lightly. You know my abilities, then why are you talking like this?"

Atul says," Dev, you don't understand. He is just like the way you were 7 years ago and this long gap is enough to create a lot of difference in our abilities."

His uncle takes a long pause and continues," The thing is that Dev, I am not taking you back so that you can give up your life fighting against Aksh or anyone else. I am taking you there because we need you. You belong there. I want you to understand that the day you feel like tired down or torn down, just let me know. We will find some alternate path to solve our problems. Dev, I don't want to lose you again; this time not for eternity."

Dev says," Uncle, I have waited for this opportunity for the last seven years. I am not going to let this slip off my hands. I am going back there and taking what really belongs to me and my people."

Dev starts his preparation while he says to his uncle pointing to the severely injured people lying on the ground," What about these people?"

Atul says," Well, they are criminals. You would have taken them down even in the city too. So, leave them here."

Dev says," Uncle, I wish to say thank you for giving me this opportunity."

His uncle says," Don't thank me too early. The thing is that because of your last acts I was forced to issue an arrest warrant in the name of Yaksh. So, when you are back as Yaksh you have to be careful both from Aksh as well as from the police department as well."

Dev says," Wow, awesome. Anything else?"

Atul nods in rejection as Dev says," Was there no warrant against my own name?"

Atul thinks for a moment and says," I got it. Are you talking about Vidya?"

Dev says," Yes, you can take it that way."

Atul says," Vidya did come to me to lodge a FIR against you but when I told her you had already left, she didn't lodge it."

Dev says," Okay. At least, someone did some good to me. By the way, how is she?"

Atul says," Well, she is heading her father's business in a good direction and is also trying her level best to take a stand against the crime but all her efforts are going in vain because no one is there to support her. Maybe, from now on she will going to have a partner along with whom she could make her stand stronger."

Dev says," Well first, I need to apologize to her."

Dev completes his packing and they both leave for the station. The uncle-son duo takes the very first bus available back to their city.

CHAPTER 27

Its early morning when they both arrive back in their home town. Finally, the wait of seven long years is over for Dev. His exile has been terminated. Dev and his uncle start walking towards their destination. After going through some unknown streets, Dev asks his uncle," Uncle, where are we heading to?"

Atul says," Straight to your house."

Dev says," Uncle, can I stay with you for sometime before going and meeting my family. I have got some butterflies in my stomach."

Atul says," Ok."

Dev says," But, uncle. I don't understand. My house is not on this street as per what I remember."

Atul says," Actually, we were headed to your new house."

Dev says," Whoa, when did I got the privilege of having multiple houses in this city?"

Atul says," Your brother bought it for your mother."

Dev says," That means, my old house will be empty."

Atul says," No one has not even touched it for the last couple of years."

Dev says," Great because I am staying there for sometime before moving in with my family."

Atul says," But, why? Come and stay with me."

Dev says," I wish to start from where I left. First I thought my family would have been there in my old house but now since its empty so I can easily stay there."

Atul says," Your wish, son. You are always welcome in my house. Whenever you feel like, you can come there."

Dev says," Yeah, I know."

They both decide to leave for their revised destinations but before leaving Atul says," Come over for a dinner tonight at my place."

Dev nods in approval and leaves. Atul too start walking towards his house.

CHAPTER 28

When Dev reaches back home, he is awe struck at the beauty of his house. Though his house was in complete ruins but still for him it was a delight to watch after such a long gap. He picks his luggage and enters his house. There is dust everywhere and the rest of the furniture is covered by long white drapes. Dev keeps his luggage in a corner and begins to clean up his house. By afternoon, he was too tired. He had cleaned up a room to rest and kitchen to cook his meals. He even gave up his dirty look. Now, he took was looking like a complete gentleman.

But the kitchen had nothing in store for him to eat. So, Dev decides to go to the market and have his afternoon meals. After returning back, Dev simply goes straight to his bed and dozes off to sleep.

It's in the late afternoon when Dev wakes up and realizes that he had to go for a dinner at his uncle's residence. He leaves his bed and rushes to the fresh room.

Dev very speedily dresses himself in his best available clothes and leaves for his uncle's residence. On the way, he decides to take some sweets as dessert. He enters a sweet shop and was perplexed to see so many sweets in the shop. The sweet shop had a mirror in front through which the entire back traffic could be easily seen. While Dev was deciding which to pick, something happened and Dev got terribly nervous. His heart started to beat like never before. He was feeling like his legs were sinking deep into the ground and he couldn't move an inch. His sixth sense made him feel that someone was standing right behind him rather someone known. Before Dev could gather all his courage to turn around, some familiar voice reaches his ear echoing his name," Dev." He understood who the person was but was too coward to turn around. His heart was getting heavy with every passing second.

Maybe the person herself recognized Dev correctly and knew that Dev will not turn around, so she herself came in front of Dev. She was none other than Vidya. Dev could not speak anything. It was a terrifying moment for Dev. The girl with whom he fell in love with, the girl whose father he murdered in cold hands was standing right in front of him.

Dev's voice was gone. He moved his lips mutely saying," I am sorry." A single stroll of tear rolls down Vidya's cheek as she lands a tight slap on Dev's face and goes away. She was crying heavily when Dev last saw her before she sped away in her car.

Dev was completely motionless until one of the vendors says to him," Are you alright, sir? Which sweet should I pack for you?"

Dev rubbing his cheek says," I got one."

Vendor could not understand what Dev was saying and Dev too was lost in the moment when Vidya slapped him. Suddenly, he comes back to the present and replies by pointing to a certain sweet to pack for him. Dev pays the bill, takes his packet of sweet and starts walking towards his uncle's residence.

During Dev's walk towards his uncle's residence, all the good memories shared with Vidya were flashing in front of him. With each passing car's flashlight, a memory flashed and faded. There are certain times when we are happy as well as sad by seeing someone. Dev was happy to get a glance of Vidya but also it made him refresh what he did to her father unknowingly.

Before, Dev could overcome all his tragedies and could gather his senses, he finds himself standing at the doorstep of his uncle's residence. He rings the door bell and waits for his uncle to open the gate for him. But, there was another surprise in store for him. The gate opens up but rather than his uncle someone else opens the door. In fact an old lady opens the door. Dev loses his grip on the sweet box after seeing the old lady. Before Dev could even recognize the old lady, another slap lands on his face; this time from the old lady. Dev whispers to himself," How many more? 2 already" referring to the two slaps from the 2 ladies.

The old lady was none other than his mother who had waited for him for the last seven years. She is the same mother who passed her every moment believing that some day she will get the privilege to see her son back. She is the mother who was dying every moment and was still keeping her last breath to see her son. And, finally here he was.

Dev was shell shocked. He expected such a kind of welcome greeting but back to back he could never dream of. This time again he says," I am sorry." He bents down to touch his mother's feet. His mother starts crying and so too Dev. They both try to wipe away each other's tears when Dev says," Why are you crying mother? This is not the time to cry but to celebrate."

His mother says," Stupid, these are tears of joy and not of sorrow. These are the tears that I have held back for so many years eagerly waiting for you. Dev, where have you been? You should have never given such a harsh punishment to your mother, Dev."

Dev too was brimming with emotions but says," Mother, I am really sorry for the troubles I gave you. I promise mother I will never leave you alone again. Please forgive me."

His mother says," You don't have to ask me for that. You are my child, Dev. I forgave you the day you left but you disappointed me when you made me wait for so long to see you again."

With this, the mother-son duo hugs each other. They were crying heavily but were happy this time. Dev's uncle Atul was seeing all this from a distance. He too got a few tears in his eyes as well. He says to Dev's mother," Stop it, at least let him come in. And also, the food is ready to serve. We talk the rest on the table."

Dev picks up the sweets box. Dev's mother holding Dev's one hand brings him inside the house. Dev says to his mother," You have got old, mother?"

His mother says," The secret to my youthfulness is my family. You were missing for the last seven years and so my beauty went down. But now since my family is complete again, I have got my secret recipe back and therefore now I will become more beautiful for my family again."

Dev says," Not only beautiful but also healthy."

His mother says," Yes, absolutely."

They both reach the dining table where the food was served to eat. Atul too joins them after bringing all the cooked meals to the table. The trio prays to God and thanks him to finally giving them the privilege to have a meal together as a re-united family.

CHAPTER 29

Dev and his mother had a lot to talk about. So, they started off asking each other while they were taking their meals. His mother asks first," So, where all have you been?"

Dev says," I have been to a lot of places rather safer places. Initially, I was enjoying the loneliness but slowly that same loneliness started to eat me from inside. I was trying to find some reason to come back home."

His mother says," So, now you need a reason to come back home?"

Dev says," Mother, after what all I did, I never imagined coming back."

His mother says," Dev, I don't want to know what all you did wrong. I just want to tell you one thing. Had you told me once about your dilemma you were facing in your life I would have definitely helped you. Anyways Dev, I really want you to start living in the present. Start a new life, Dev."

Dev says," That's maybe why I am here back again. So, now you tell me how are you and how is Pallav?"

His mother says," Well, I am doing fine but your brother is doing great. He continued the father's business and now he is earning rich dividends. Had he knew you are back here; he would have definitely been here among us tonight. He really missed you a lot, Dev."

Dev says," That means Pallav do not knows I am back in town?"

His mother knows," Neither did I till I saw you at the door. Your uncle came in the morning at our house to invite us for a get together and he promised us a surprise package but your brother was busy in the evening, so he sent me alone. By the way, where have you been staying and why don't you join us and stay with us in our new house?"

Dev says," I am not staying with uncle but I am staying at our old house."

His mother," Now, you have crossed the limits Dev. You are coming with me and I don't want to hear any excuses."

Dev just couldn't oppose his mother rather he didn't want to oppose her. He too was dying to meet his family at the earliest and what a surprise it has been. They all complete their dinner. Dev helps his uncle wash the utensils while his mother cleans up the left over. After that, they relish their dessert together and enjoyed recollecting their fond memories.

It was late in the night when Dev and his mother decide to leave. While leaving, Dev goes to his uncle and says," Thanks a lot, uncle."

His uncle says," You want to thank me for this then do hell with your thank you. I wanted you to realize that people still believe in you. Now, you go and enjoy this moment with your family because sooner or later you will have to get back to work."

Dev hugs his uncle, wishes him good night and leaves with his mother.

CHAPTER 30

While the mother-son duo was driving back to their new home, they first went to their old house from where they picked up Dev's luggage. When they reached their old house, Dev's mother tells the driver to help Dev get his luggage while she waited in the car itself. Dev along with the driver went in and within some time they both came out carrying Dev's luggage.

On reaching the entrance of the new house, Dev was too shocked to see the enormity of their new residence. It was not a house; it was a palace. The house was as big as nothing else; it was beautiful, enormous and traditionally built. The house had terrific lawns surrounding it from all the four sides. There were steep high walls on the sides so as to give a sense of security to the residents. The security was at its best. Not even a single person could enter or leave the premises without getting noticed. This was all from the outside.

The car straight away drove through the front door and stopped at the main gate of the house. They both got down from the car and the driver pulls out Dev's luggage, goes inside the house and keeps it in a corner in the guest room. Dev helps his mother and they both enter their new house. It was as beautiful from inside as it was from the outside.

They had just entered when Dev's mother asks one of the servants," Is Pallav home?"

The servant nods in approval. Dev's mother further says to the servant," Go and call Pallav. Tell him that there is a special guest who has come to see him."

The servant goes straight to Pallav's room and gives him his mother's message. Pallav comes out of his room and what he sees next surprises him completely.

Dev was thinking only one thing how will his brother react after seeing him. What if even a gap of seven years could not heal the bitterness between the two brothers?

The two brothers were staring at each other. Dev could easily see that Pallav had heavily built himself. Dev thinking of another welcome greeting in the form of another high intensity slap from his brother could dismantle his jaw forever didn't move a single step. Rather, Pallav come speeding towards Dev and on the contrary gives Dev a tight hug. Dev was surprised and happy too that at least his brother didn't slap him.

Dev could easily see the happiness in the eyes of Pallav. For the first time in his life his brother had accepted him. Even that acceptance had created doubts in Dev's mind. Maybe, his brother had accepted him because now he too was a criminal. Or is it something else. Dev was thinking all this when Pallav says," Dev, where are you lost? Come, grab a seat."

Dev along with his mother and Pallav sit on the well furnished sofas. They were all sitting on different sofas when their mother calls them to sit on one single sofa together. She had missed this moment for so long. She was dying to have this moment back again in her life.

Pallav and Dev exchange pleasantries when Pallav asks Dev," So Dev, what have you decided of your future? What will you do now?"

Dev says," I have taken a lot of rest, so I am eager to get some work in my hands."

Pallav says," But brother, when you left, you also left your graduation incomplete."

Dev says," Yeah, I know but I suppose there might be some work where they require your capabilities and not the degrees."

Pallav says," Ok, well if you don't find some you are always welcome to join me in our father's business."

Dev says," Yeah, definitely. But, I would love to try some before joining you in the business. Till that time, I would prefer breeding on my brother's wealth."

The trio breaks into laughter. It was already midnight. So they all decide to go to bed and talk the rest in the days to come. The servant had already prepared the guest room for Dev to take some rest. They all wish each other good night and heads straight to their rooms to take a hearty sleep.

Dev fell into sound sleep the moment he touched his bed. He woke up late in the morning when his mother called him for lunch. It was already about to get afternoon, so his mother decided to wake up his son by herself. She comes to his room, removes the curtains and says," Wake up, Kumbhkaran. It's already afternoon. I am preparing your special food. So, please wake up."

Dev yawningly wakes up and gets up from his bed after further insistence from his mother. He was tired to think anything else and goes straight to wash room to take a bath. After having a bath and putting up some decent clothes, Dev takes the lunch with his mother and his brother. His mother pointing towards Pallav says," See, your brother is following your footsteps. He too has started to wake up late in the morning."

It was a sudden shock that sent shivers down the spine of Dev and he was now completely out of his sleeps. Dev knowingly asks his brother," Why do you wake up so late, brother?"

Pallav says," Actually, I am always busy with my business till late in the night. So, I am not able to sleep well in the night."

Their mother interrupts in between and says," Your brother works too much now a day. But now since you are here, your presence could relieve some load from his shoulders for some time."

Dev says," I really appreciate Pallav working so hard and I am definitely looking forward for relieving him from his job."

Pallav interrupts and says," Well, for now I am enjoying my job. I already told you if you wish to join me, then you are most welcome. It will in fact provide a hand in my work."

Dev says," Well, this reminds me that I have to go to look for a new job. I will try and find some job which meets my caliber and potential."

The trio finishes off their lunch. Dev decides to leave for the city while Pallav decides to go back to his work. Their mother decides to rest for some time in the afternoon.

CHAPTER 31

Dev takes a bag in which he puts all his essential equipments and leaves for the city. Though he told his family that he was going in search of a job but in reality he was going somewhere else. He heads straight to his old house.

It was mid afternoon, so the rush in the streets was also less. Dev before going to his old house goes first to a cloth shop. He purchases some fine cloth material and then heads straight to his house. Upon reaching his house, he goes straight to the room that he cleaned up yesterday. He has already decided by now that he will operate everything from this place only.

Dev begins his work but first decides to find all the essential things he need at the start. He recognizes that he needs to study the working areas of his brother because his brother is the only source to Aksh. And most importantly he needs a new costume.

Dev decides that he will start following his brother from tonight onwards. He leaves the house once he finishes his work and heads straight to a new destination. After some time, Dev reaches his destination; 22 Malabar Coast. The building was still the same. The moment Dev saw that building he recalled some of the very unfriendly memories of his past.

But gathering some strength he enters the building. He goes straight to the receptionist and asks her," Excuse me, can I have the privilege to meet Vidya Bansal, please."

The receptionist says," Sir, do you have an appointment to meet her?"

Dev says," Well, I don't have it but if you tell your ma'am that someone named Dev is here to meet her, then definitely I will going to get an appointment on the spot."

The receptionist says," Ok Sir, please have a seat. I shall convey your message to Vidya ma'am."

The receptionist picks up the phone while Dev roams around the lobby. The receptionist tells her ma'am that someone named Dev is here to meet her. Vidya asks to the receptionist," Is he all alone?"

The receptionist answers," Yes."

Vidya says," Then, tell him that I am busy in a meeting. Tell him to wait for an hour. And if he holds on then after that one hour, send him on the 19th floor office."

The receptionist was puzzled because neither Vidya was busy in a meeting and nor the 19th floor was operational anymore. It was completely abandoned.

The receptionist says," But, ma'am."

Before she complete her question, the reply came from the other side," Do what you are asked to do." And Vidya hangs up the phone.

The receptionist calls for Dev who was wandering in the lobby. She tells him," Ma'am Vidya is actually busy in a meeting. It will last at least an hour. She can meet you after that only. So, would you be interested in setting an appointment with her once she completes her meeting?"

Dev says," Ok, as she wish. Give me an appointment."

Dev was sitting in the waiting room when after an hour the receptionist calls his name. It was late in the afternoon and the sun was about to touch the horizon. Dev reaches the reception. The receptionist says, "Mr. Dev, you are permitted to meet Ms. Vidya on the 19th floor."

Dev was a little shocked. He asks the receptionist," But, it's written there that your ma'am's office is on 10th floor. Then why I am meeting her on the 19th floor?"

The receptionist says," Sir, ma'am asked me to send you there. So, I am sending you there. Would you please go and meet her now because you are running out of time."

Forcibly, Dev enters the lift and goes straight to the 19th floor. He could now easily presume what Vidya was doing with him.

CHAPTER 32

Dev reaches the 19th floor. He leaves the lift and heads towards the only lighted area of the floor. The 19th floor was completely abandoned. Not even a single human soul could be seen on the floor. The lights were too dim to see the way but Dev could easily make his way for he knew this place and especially this floor.

The lights were on in just a single office. So, Dev starts walking towards it. Upon reaching the office, he knocks on the door but realizes the door was already open. He quietly moves in and sees Vidya dressed in a beautiful traditional sari standing right beside the broken glass window.

The furniture, the surroundings everything was just the same in the office the way Dev left it when he murdered Vidya's father here. No repair work has been done over here.

Vidya realizing that Dev was here turns around. They both stand staring at each other. They were dumb from their mouths but their eyes were conveying a thousand words to each other. Vidya starts the conversation by saying," So, remember anything of this place?"

Dev says," Oh, come on Vidya. You also know what all happened here."

Vidya says," Why? You have a lot of daring to do it but cannot dare to speak about it."

Dev says," Vidya, calm down. I just want your forgiveness and that's all. I will leave after that."

Vidya says," You want my forgiveness?"

Dev says," Yes, I do."

Vidya says," Do you know what Dev the day you murdered my father I went to the police station. There your uncle told me that you left feeling guilty for your wrong doings. That day I thought that you had self punished yourself as well as all of us by leaving us shattered. I was too fired up but I soon realized that this anger will neither bring my father back and nor you back from your exile. So, that day I decided two things. Firstly, I decided that I will going to prove to you that you are no longer needed in my life. I can stand up on my own and I can fight against any kind of injustice. First I started by applying this on me but then sooner I realized that the whole city was suffering because of some or the other form of injustice and therefore I decided to take a stand for them too using all my resources."

Dev was patiently listening to what Vidya was saying. Vidya continues by saying," Secondly, I decided that this exile was a kind of self punishment. This does not fulfill my hunger to avenge you. I have been eagerly waiting for the day when I myself can harm you in a big way. I am not going to leave you, Dev. This hatred that I have for you will burn forever inside me."

Dev was dumb struck. He knew it would be hard to get what he wanted from her but still he tries. Dev says," Vidya, don't do this to yourself. You cannot even think leave alone feel the burden that I have shouldered for so many years for my single wrong doing. So, please don't do this. This revenge feeling benefits no one. But still if you are so adamant, then tell me what do you want from me in return of your forgiveness?"

Vidya says," Since, your father is already dead so, I would like to kill your mother. This will make both of our accounts equal."

Dev was shell shocked as to what Vidya was saying. Dev in a very authorative tone says," Are you out of your mind? I will not allow you to do that."

Vidya says," Hey man!! Relax!! I am just kidding. Dev, I want to avenge my father's death and one day I will take it what I want from you. That day, you will be forgiven."

Dev who by now had lost the hope of an immediate forgiveness, stone heartedly says," I will be eagerly waiting for that day to come."

Vidya says," Good, be prepared for it."

Dev stares at Vidya for a moment when she says," Now, what are you waiting for? Just get out."

Dev was about to leave when he goes close to Vidya and says," A very happy belated birthday to you. May you get what you wish for."

With this, Dev leaves. Yesterday, when Vidya met Dev at the sweet's shop, Dev was in complete shock and could not recall anything. But, in the night time he remembered it was Vidya's birthday. That's why she came to the sweets shop to buy some sweets to celebrate her birthday all alone like she has been doing for the last seven years or so but she discovered Dev who used to be once the sweetest of the sweets in her life.

CHAPTER 33

Dev reaches back home late in the evening. He freshens himself up by taking a bath and then goes straight to the dining hall to have something to eat. His mother was waiting for him so that they both can have dinner together. They were about to sit on their respective chairs when Dev asks her mother," Should I call Pallav too?"

His mother replies back," Actually, he went out with some business work and he will not return back before midnight."

Suddenly, Dev became conscious about Pallav but still hiding his curiosity, he says to his mother," Ok, then let's have dinner."

Dev wanted to go after Pallav immediately but he doesn't know where his brother went. So, he decided to wait for another opportunity to come by his way. Dev says to his mother," The food is delicious. By the way, do you know where Pallav's office is or where he goes to do his business?"

His mother says," I don't know anything about his whereabouts, Dev. I just know he goes late in the evening and comes late after midnight and also he goes every alternate day."

Dev was happy at not only the delicious food but also because he got at least some useful information about his brother's busines. He decides that he will follow his brother the very next time he goes out. Dev now had almost 48 hours to decide upon his plan of action.

The very next morning Dev leaves for his old house where his base for all this operations was settled. He sees his uncle on the door waiting for him. Actually, Dev himself had called him to discuss the strategy. They both enter the house and heads straight to Dev's room. Dev asks his uncle," So, what have you got for me?"

His uncle says," I don't have much but I can tell you one thing. Now days it is not easy even to find Aksh leave alone to think of taking him down."

Dev says," So, what do you propose?"

Atul says," I would just simply say make the people feel your presence as Yaksh. This will most probably force Pallav to call Aksh soon or the other way round is that straight away attack your brother. The problem with second option is that it has a high chance of failure."

Dev asks his uncle," Why?"

His uncle says," Because, maybe when you attack your brother, at that time Aksh may not be present and forcefully you will have to be contended with your brother only. Therefore, I would prefer you taking one of the headquarters of your brother down when he is not there."

Dev says," Yeah, it's a good choice. But, we will have to wait till I find his one of the headquarters. My mother told me that Pallav visits his sites on every alternate day. So, that means it can easily provide us with a big window of opportunity to strike any of his sites because on a single day he can visit only a limited number of his sites only. Therefore, first we have to trace him for a week before we could strike him."

Atul says," And what if I already know on which days he visits his which all sites?"

Dev says," Whoa. Then tell me, we can strike him tomorrow itself."

Atul says," Ok, I will give you the name of his sites."

Atul hands over the information to Dev. While Dev was busy going through the documents, he jokingly says to his uncle," You just make sure that your police arrive on the scene only when I had finished my work like it happens in most of our Hindi movies."

Atul says," Hey, man!! It's not a movie where police will arrive after the action has happened. They will arrive only when it is required. But still if you insist, I will try and postpone our arrival on the scene."

Finally, after going through the entire documents, Dev says," Ok, so here is our plan of action. Since, Pallav visited his one of the site yesterday itself and my mother told me he visits his sites every alternate day, so that means we can strike today itself. But, there is a problem."

Atul says," What is it now? You have all the required information."

Dev says," Are you really confident that Pallav's business runs throughout the week and his visit every alternate day doesn't mean that for the rest of the days there is no wrong happening out there on the other sites simultaneously?"

Atul says," See, Pallav has become so strong and powerful that now he seldom visits his sites. He leaves his work in the hands of his most trusted people and he visits these sites every alternate days just to check their working."

Dev says," We can attack them right now itself."

Atul says," No, no. Attack them in night."

Dev says," But, why?"

Atul says," Because their business operates at its peak in the night time itself. They smuggle and transport their drugs throughout the city in the night only without any fear. So, if you wish to make them fear you, you need to attack them when they work without any fear."

Dev says," Ok, in the night."

They both agree and wait for sun to go down.

CHAPTER 34

The sun crosses the horizon and finally signals the end of a long wait as Dev prepares himself for a much awaited showdown. His uncle leaves him at his house and goes straight to his station to wait. Dev already told his uncle that he would at most need an hour to do his work and after that his uncle along with his team can arrive on the scene.

Dev too leaves for his target in casual clothes. He stops way ahead of his destination and finds a suitable place to do a changeover. Finally, Yaksh is back. The long wait of seven years is over.

Yaksh reaches his target and straight away attacks the local goons surrounding the perimeter and beats them all one by one. Before the goons that were working inside could even come to know what all was happening outside, Yaksh breaks in with a bang. Everyone is stunned and ice frozen to the ground. They couldn't have imagined this happening even in wildest of their dreams as well.

What follows next cost them dearly. They try to attack Yaksh but either they didn't knew it or were just taking a chance to save themselves but the more harder they tried the easier it became for Yaksh.

It was just 5 minutes within which Yaksh had finished his job. Every single goon was on the ground. He was about to leave the scene but before leaving he was still left to do one more task. He captures one of the local goons, wakes him up and asks," Where is Aksh?"

The goon replies back," Don't even try finding him."

Yaksh says," Why? He already ran away."

The goon replies back," Because what all you have done today, after this he will himself come chasing you."

Yaksh lands a tight punch on his face and says" Ok, then I will wait for him but by that time I want you to do me favor. You go and tell your boss that either he leave this city or surrender because when I will go hunting him and which I definitely will; he will be left with no place to hide. I give him six days to decide and act and after that no one will be able to save neither your boss nor your powerful ally Aksh. So, go and tell them that I am back. I am back to take my city back from your dirty hands."

Yaksh leaves the goon and the goon runs away. Yaksh too leaves the spot, goes to a safe place, once again do a changeover and then calls his uncle saying," I have done my job. You are up next." Dev hangs up the phone and leaves for his house. He knew that he had made a move. Now, he has to just wait and watch when Aksh steps out.

An hour later Dev's uncle Atul and his police force arrives on the scene and sees various goons lying on the ground injured very badly. They easily discovered the drugs and seized the entire site. The police department too was shocked as to what had happened there.

The goons who were a little conscious were taking just a single name," Yaksh." Police force was still completely out of any idea because they had no evidence to verify who had the daring to do this large scale damage to Sarraf's business. Going by what goons were saying, they were a little confident that maybe Yaksh who they knew as their savior is back again. But, in reality they were not willing to believe it. They were not willing to believe in the same Yaksh again who back stabbed them seven years ago.

The newspapers flooded with the news of someone daring to take Sarraf's business by attacking one of his main sites yesterday night. Some newspapers even claimed that after seeing the damage done single handedly, it could be someone very powerful behind all this. They even pointed out at Yaksh too but they too no had photos, no videos nothing to support this. The police force was keeping the accident report close to them and was not willing to give any information to the media.

The very following day an urgent meeting was called upon by the mayor. The meeting also included various politicians and higher police officials. They wanted to discuss about what happened yesterday night. They not only had to answer their senior but also Pallav because they were a puppet in his hands. So, they were required to act immediately and wisely.

The meeting started and all had just one question in their minds," Who to be blamed for yesterday's encounter?"

The mayor started the meeting by saying," Just be quiet. We are about to start the meeting. Our police report says that Yaksh was behind all this. The report sets its base on the goons continuously recalling Yaksh's name at the scene."

The mayor continues says," Do anyone among you have anyone else to blame?"

One of the wise man says," Maybe, this mafia is fighting within them."

The mayor says," Ok, this could also be an alternative to yesterday's incident." The moment mayor stops, his PA knocks on the door and enters the room.

He says to the mayor," The video tapes are ready. You can have a look at them."

The mayor announce," Finally, we have it. The video tapes of yesterday's incident are here and now it will be clear who is behind all this?"

The mayor instructs his servant to play the tape. Once going through the tape everyone was shell shocked to see Yaksh back but in a different look. But, they were confident it was Yaksh only.

After going through the tape, everyone was dumb struck. The mayor says," It's really confusing. The person who back stabbed us in the past is back again to clean up his wrong doings. It does not fit in."

Dev's uncle Atul too was present in the meeting when he says," Who knows he is here to save us. He is our last hope in this hopeless system."

The mayor says," We cannot trust him. Though he did a wonderful job yesterday but it's hard to believe in him again. I do accept this that maybe he could be our last chance to get this city cleaned up but I cannot do this by keeping my police force lives at stake. So, the arrest warrant which was issued in the name of Yaksh is to be hold good. If he is the same Yaksh that we used to know then first he needs to answer all the wrong which he did to us. Then only, we will change our minds and decision."

A press statement was announced confirming that Yaksh was behind yesterday's act and still his arrest warrant will hold good till the authorities do not get confidence upon trusting Yaksh again.

CHAPTER 35

Pallav was shell shocked. He too just can't believe what happened yesterday night. Pallav gets fired up when the messenger transfers the message word to word the way Yaksh told him to his boss. He decides to call Aksh back to work just for a cover. Pallav was now eager and curious to meet Yaksh. He decides to wait for the next six days because after that he will himself go hunting Yaksh.

Dev was going through the day with his daily routine work. He was not at all disturbed the way Pallav was. He was relaxed and looked completely calm. He too was waiting for the next six days to pass so that he can openly take Aksh down.

The deadline was of six days. But, neither did anything absurd. Pallav continued with his business visits every alternate day and Dev as Yaksh was taking Pallav's business site one by one. In the six days deadline, Yaksh had taken almost 8 sites and beaten at least 100 local goons present on various sites during his random raids. The local goons too started to fear him. They all pleaded Pallav to call Aksh back soon.

Everyday news flashed of Yaksh taking the goons down like old days. Yaksh's act instilled courage in the hearts of the dumb and deaf people who wanted to fight for their own freedom. One of these included Vidya too. She was flying now and was trying to make people realize that their dark days are over. A new morning has arrived.

It's time to wake up and act. Her efforts didn't go in vain and people started to respond. Crime started to curb as goons started to fear.

Finally, the sixth day was over. The deadline ended. The seventh day started with a heavy weather. There were clear signs of a heavy downpour at any moment in the day. Maybe, they too were indicating towards the thunder that was about to happen tonight.

As usual, the entire day passed by. In late evening, Pallav and Dev both left the house making certain excuses to their mother. Dev went straight to his old house, did a changeover and left straight to the site which Pallav was supposed to visit today. Upon reaching his proposed target site, Yaksh stays at some distance and tries to find Aksh but he was still missing. Yaksh was frustrated now. He was in a dilemma whether to attack the goons or not since Aksh was still missing.

Where is Aksh?

But, Yaksh had plans for the day. So as per what he had decided, he attacks the site by taking every single of the guard that was securing the perimeter. Pallav knew that Yaksh had arrived but was acting completely normal. Yaksh breaks into the main building and to his surprise there was no one except Pallav himself.

Yaksh was moved by witnessing the daring of Pallav. They both were standing at a distance. Yaksh wanted Aksh and not Pallav. So, he didn't make a move.

Seeing Yaksh being motionless, Pallav breaks the silence by saying," Whoa! Whoa! A new costume; you surprised me."

Yaksh was still not ready to speak a single word. He feared that his brother might recognize him by his voice. So, he decides to stay silent and wait for Aksh to come soon. Pallav continues," What? You are waiting for someone?"

This time Yaksh nods but doesn't speak anything. Pallav says," So, what now? You are going to arrest me?"

Finally, Yaksh with a heavy voice says," Where is Aksh?"

Pallav laughs but this time he does not respond. Yaksh swiftly goes to Pallav and lands a tight slap on Pallav's face. Pallav falls on the ground. Yaksh again repeats his question," Do not waste my time, you are no use to me. Tell me where is Aksh?"

Pallav gets up. Yaksh holds him by his collar before Pallav says," Ok, let me tell you."

Pallav takes a pause. Suddenly, Aksh flies in with great speed from the right side of Yaksh and with his great momentum takes Yaksh away with him in a flipper. Pallav says to himself," Talk of the devil and here he is. You should have at least allowed me to complete my answer."

Without caring what Pallav was muttering to him, Aksh and Yaksh lands together straight into the middle of the city. It indeed was a high impact landing.

They both tear apart the road where they both land. The vehicles that were on the road became fireballs and were now flying all across the streets. Some landed in the shops and some in the buildings but wherever they landed, they created more fire to erupt from everywhere. The fire alarms went on and the entire city was echoing the same noise. People were forced to leave their offices and come out on the streets.

They were horrified to see Aksh and Yaksh because their landing was such that it appeared like as if some meteor has crashed. The news spreads like fire and the noise of sirens could be heard easily coming from all the directions; some of them were that of police while some of fire brigade and some of ambulances.

CHAPTER 36

By the time people gathered in the streets, Aksh and Yaksh were regaining their consciousness. They both were lying on one another since they landed together. Yaksh gets up first and separates himself from Aksh. Aksh was still lying on the ground. Yaksh asks from the nearby crowd," Is everyone safe?"

Before anyone could answer, an announcement is made on the megaphone by the police force," Yaksh, step down and surrender yourself."

Yaksh was feeling disgusted. He was about to turn around when Aksh throws an ice cream cycle shop straight at Yaksh. Yaksh tears the ice cream shop into two by his bare hands. Aksh says to Yaksh," You want to fight for them when they crazily want you dead."

Yaksh looks towards the public and confidently replies back," Yes, I do." The entire public gives a round of applause and formally welcomes their hero back into their lives and into their city.

Police forces too sensing danger decides to step back. Aksh says," Ok, then. Since, you yourself have chosen to be my opponent so, I am forced to show no mercy when I kill you."

With this, Aksh makes his move and lands tight punches on Yaksh. Yaksh goes flying by and lands in one of the buildings. But, he soon regains himself and flies back to the same place unhurt. Aksh was now fired up. He grabs one of the persons and throws him towards Yaksh. Yaksh dives and tries to catch the person. Yaksh dives forward and successfully catches the person but in time he finds himself getting trapped. By the time, Yaksh dived and safely protected the person, Aksh found a heavy vehicle standing by. He picks it up and throws straight at Yaksh. This time Yaksh had no time to duck or even react. He gets hit by the truck and lands far away in the street. The truck catches fire immediately as it lands in the street. Yaksh was still in the fire when the truck explodes sending Yaksh high in the air. Aksh sensing an opportunity grabs Yaksh in mid air by his leg and smashes Yaksh in various buildings while Aksh continue flying across the various buildings at a great speed.

Yaksh was now getting bored up. He decides to end this. While they were in air, Yaksh gains balance and hits hard at the hand from which Aksh was holding Yaksh's leg. Suddenly, out of pain Aksh leaves Yaksh's leg and Yaksh loses a little altitude in the air before regaining his control. He flies to the same height where Aksh was screaming in pain.

Yaksh says to Aksh," You have really disappointed me. You are so weak."

Yaksh picks up a big piece of marble from the adjacent building and throws straight at Aksh. Aksh who was already in pain gets hit by the fast approaching piece and before he could even gain control in the air, Yaksh lands a tight hit from the top which lands him straight into the ground.

Aksh was biting the dust while Yaksh was still in the air. Yaksh was hoping for some fight back from Aksh but soon he realizes it was not possible. Yaksh mutters to him,"

That's it. That's why uncle Atul wanted Yaksh. Oh boy!! You must be kidding me. That was seriously so easy."

Yaksh safely lands on the ground and walks straight towards the hole where Aksh was lying. He jumps into the hole and throws Aksh out. Aksh was completely unconscious. Pointing towards Aksh, Yaksh says to the public and the police," He belongs to you. You all are free now."

The police force start moving towards Aksh to capture him. Dev's uncle was also present on the scene. But, there was one thing that Yaksh wanted to know. He wanted to know who is really behind Aksh's mask. He moves towards Aksh and was about to remove Aksh's mask when suddenly he disappears before removing the mask. Everyone looks here and there in search of Yaksh but he was gone with the speed of light.

CHAPTER 37

Yaksh disappears in thin smoke and within a few moments later Aksh appears amidst the public and says," The real party begins now."

Saying this, Aksh too leaves the public in deep shock. Actually, when Yaksh was about to remove the mask of unconscious Aksh, another Aksh hits him at a great speed and Yaksh goes flying by. Aksh do not go with Yaksh but stays back to announce the beginning of real fun and party.

Everyone was stunned. They could not believe what they were witnessing. Aksh was lying in front of them and another Aksh was standing as powerful as anything else. What the hell is happening? They were just too shocked to see the duplicate Aksh.

The general public who was shocked now also started to worry about Yaksh. Aksh flies in the same direction in which he hit Yaksh and the rest of the police, public and various other officials follow him too.

Meanwhile, Yaksh lands in an old factory. He removes off his mask to gain control of his senses. He mutters to himself," What's happening? How many Aksh are there?"

Suddenly, the lights are turned on and there is a noise of vehicles halting outside the factory. Sensing danger, Dev puts on his mask back again and prepares his guard. All the doors are sent wide open and people carrying heavy weapons in their hand start to enter the factory from all sides. Yaksh watches the armored people starting to surround him.

He shakes his head in disapproval to fight them when suddenly Aksh flies in by breaking the ceiling and lands in front of him. Aksh says to Yaksh," So, you are enjoying the party?"

Yaksh replies back," Bring me the real fight. I can beat any number of your people like this" referring to the armored people.

Aksh says," They are not here to fight you. They are here to see me defeating you."

Yaksh says," It's good to think like that but thinking and doing are two different things. Don't you feel ashamed of yourself; first you robbed my costume, then I don't know how many of you exist but all of you are using the same costume again and again."

Yaksh continues," Common on, man! Tell me who the real Aksh is. Are you also not a duplicate one because the previous one was no match for me? And, if you are the real one, then it would be great otherwise you too will be lying on the ground like your previous dear buddy in the streets."

Aksh was patiently listening to Yaksh but now he too was losing his cool. He says," Who will be lying on the ground only time will tell?"

They both were getting furious to end this. Yaksh makes his first move and lands a couple of punches on Aksh's body. Aksh was completely unmoved. Seeing this, Yaksh lands a full power hit on Aksh's jaws and this time Aksh goes flying high in the sky. Yaksh was at last feeling confident that he was powerful than this Aksh too but he too was to be proved wrong.

Aksh although got hit but it was not too powerful enough. He gains control in mid air and with full speed flies back into the factory and lands a tight hit on Yaksh with all his momentum. The impact was so hard that Yaksh lands deep into the ground creating a 10 feet deep cavity in the ground. Aksh now start firing punches on Yaksh's body. Yaksh was so severely hit that he could not revolt leave alone protect himself against the power hitting of Aksh. He had almost given up his spirit to fight back.

Aksh stops hitting Yaksh once he too realizes that Yaksh is almost broken. Aksh goes near to Yaksh and sits beside him and says," So, you see now who is lying on the ground?"

Aksh looks at Yaksh and then continues," Now, you listen to me carefully. The earlier Aksh you fought was just a dummy. I am the real Aksh."

Yaksh tries to stand but Aksh lands another tight hit on Yaksh's leg. Yaksh was now completely down. Now, he cannot even think to stand. Aksh says to Yaksh," Start counting your last breath."

Aksh and Yaksh were both in the hole. It was not possible for the surrounding armored people to see what was happening inside the cavity. The general public, police had all gathered there but were not allowed to go in the factory by the armored people. Aksh had already told his men that he doesn't want any kind of distraction.

Aksh says to Yaksh," Now, before I kill you and end this tale, I have a plan for you. The problem is that we have not introduced ourselves to each other properly. We know each other by name but we do not know who we really are? So, let's begin with you."

Aksh goes near to Yaksh, bends down and takes his hand towards Yaksh's mask. Yaksh tries to stop him by pleading him not to do it. But, Aksh was dying to see who Yaksh really is.

Finally, Aksh removes Yaksh's mask. The moment Aksh removes the mask; he pushes Yaksh away from him. It was looking like Aksh has been paralyzed after coming to know who is behind the Yaksh's mask. But, indeed Aksh was completely shocked to see Dev behind the mask of Yaksh. Sensing a window of opportunity, Yaksh gathers all his leftover strength, snatches his mask and flies away.

The public standing outside the factory sees their hero flying away in a high speed. Moments later, Aksh too flies by but in opposite direction.

No one knew what all have happened inside the factory. Slowly, the public too starts leaving the site. The police capture the unconscious Aksh and take him into their custody.

Yaksh didn't have much power to fly back to a safe place. He picks up his casual clothes and all his essential equipments and flies far away from the city. After flying for some time, he crashes himself in a cropland. With all the left over strength, Yaksh does a changeover. Moments later when Dev was trying hard to return back to his old house, his phone rings up. It was his uncle calling.

Dev was too hurt that he cancelled the phone. The phone again rings and again it was his uncle who was calling. This time Dev picks up the phone. His uncle says," Dev, where are you? Come home right now. Your mother is very sick."

Dev was hurt very badly but could easily sense what all would happen to him now. Aksh now knows who really is behind the mask of Yaksh. He can do anything to harm Dev. What if Aksh tells all this to his boss Pallav? A hundred thoughts were going through Dev's minds. Dev now not only has to protect his city but also his dear ones too including his mother, Pallav, Vidya and his uncle.

Dev now has two options; either he himself go hunting Aksh right now at full remaining strength or get his dear ones protected first and wait for Aksh to strike. Dev thinks deeply and realizes since Aksh works for Pallav, he would have definitely told Pallav about Yaksh. Since, Pallav too will be in grief over their mother's dying state, he will not order strike on Dev at this crucial stage. That means, Dev has some time to heal up his wounds and prepare himself to end Aksh.

Dev hurriedly reaches back home. A lot of people had gathered in their house as if his mother was already declared dead. Dev's wounds could be easily seen as he was limping and walking. He goes straight to the room where his mother was lying. She was clearly taking her last breath. Pallav and his uncle Atul were already present in that room. On seeing Dev, his uncle goes to Dev to support him but like old days Pallav was unmoved.

Dev asks his uncle," Uncle, why are we not taking my mother to the hospital?"

His uncle says," Doctors have already told us that anytime she can leave us. It's already too late."

Two tears roll by Dev's cheeks. His uncle says to him," Your mother's last wish is to talk to you alone. That's why I called you to come at the earliest."

Dev's uncle Atul signals Pallav to leave Dev and his mother alone for some time. After they had left, Dev goes close to his mother and sits beside her. His mother tries to open her eyes. She sees Dev and says," Dev, my dear son. You look terrible."

Dev says," Mother, we can discuss all this later. You need to take some rest right now."

His mother says," Later, you will only be able to talk to my ghost and Dev I don't need rest. I think you do. Dev, look at yourself. It appears as if you are fighting a war. Save yourself, Dev. It's too much. I can't see you dying too early. Dev, at least give me the privilege to see your children playing with you not on earth but through heaven itself. Please Dev, I request you to pay heed to a dying person's words."

His mother continues," I want to thank you, Dev. You didn't made me witness that much proposed day when I would had been forced to chose between my two sons. Dev, thank you. I didn't tell you who I would have supported if that day ever came in my life. You know who it would have been?"

Dev says," Definitely Pallav."

His mother says," Why do you think so, Dev?"

Dev replies," Because he is the weaker one among the two of us."

His mother says," No, it's you Dev. I would have definitely taken your side, Dev. You tried so hard to make Pallav understand not to harm his own life but your every try; your every sacrifice went in vain. Dev, I know what Pallav does in his business but I never had the courage to admit it."

Dev was shell shocked. Dev says," You knew it, then why didn't you tell me?"

His mother says," Because when you returned back, I didn't wanted to lose you again. Had I told you about Pallav, you would have again tried everything to save him. And in doing so, I would have again lost you. But, now I really feel that I have failed. You have again degraded your life saving this worse city."

Dev says," Mother, I need to fulfill everyone's needs and not someone's selfish greed."

His mother says," I admire you for your philosophy. These thinking of your make you so much different form all of us. I am proud of you Dev that you have the courage to stand even when all the chips are down. I really appreciate that. Dev, you are my greatest asset."

Dev was now crying too heavily but he was satisfied and contended that his mother is happy with the way he has been leading his life. Moments later, Dev realizes that his mother has stopped breathing. Dev takes a heavy breath and closes the eyes of his mother forever. Dev leaves the room and informs his brother that their mother is no more. She is dead now. This time Pallav too breaks down heavily.

CHAPTER 38

The two brothers along with the help of other members carry their mother's body to the cremation ground. Since, Pallav was the elder brother so he gives fire to the cremation. After the cremation ceremony was over, everyone left except Pallav, Dev and their uncle.

Dev and Atul were standing together while Pallav was standing just opposite to them. Dev walk towards Pallav to give condolence to his brother. Pallav asks his brother," You look seriously injured. Are you all right?"

Dev could easily see the virtual emotional face of Pallav. He too replies back," I am feeling much better than ever I have felt in my entire life."

Pallav was taken aback. He says," By the way, who did this to you?"

Dev says," Actually, I got involved with a wrong company."

Pallav says," Beware Dev. This time you escaped but every time it might not be possible for you to escape your fate."

Dev says," I should not be worried about that when you are by my side."

Pallav didn't know what to say. He simply smiles and lovingly puts a hand on Dev's face and hugs him.

Pallav leaves Dev and his uncle all alone. It was about to get dawn. Dev too decides to leave. He leaves with his uncle to the latter's residence. When they reach Atul's house, Dev had fallen asleep. He was too tired after what all happened yesterday night and was in deep shock upon losing his mother too. Atul wakes his son saying," Reached home, Dev. Get up and take some rest."

Dev wakes up and says," No, I have no time to rest. It's time to act and not sit back and wait. I have to be out there."

Atul insists but Dev was adamant. They both knew it all ends within the next 24 hours. Either Dev will not see tomorrow's morning or Aksh will not. One of them will have to vanish today. Dev steps out of the car. He goes straight into the house. While Atul prepares something to eat, Dev takes a bath. He comes up dressed again and ready to go out there.

Atul serves him the breakfast and they both have their breakfast together. Atul could easily see the pain from which Dev was suffering. Dev was physically as well as mentally hurt. Atul says to him," Dev, at least heal up your wounds. Then take Aksh out."

Dev says," By then, it would be too late. By then, I would lose many dear ones."

Atul says," And what if I lose you? Dev, I told you earlier itself that I am not bringing you back so that one day I will be forced to permanently lose you. Dev, I don't want you to do this. Just leave all this, Dev. Today, I am saying this to you: Go, run away, Dev. Aksh will going to kill you."

Atul breaks into a cry. Dev was now getting even weaker. He says," Uncle, don't make me weak. I want you to trust me. I am taking him down today at any cost. Just believe in me. I promise you today even your Gods also cannot stop me from killing Aksh. I need to end this."

Atul had no words left to persuade Dev to give up this fight. He simply says," Dev, just keep in your mind that I am always standing by you. No matter what happens today, I will be here for you. I believe in you son." Atul was trying to hold back his tears but he could not stop them from flowing.

Dev dressed himself as Yaksh again and was ready to leave and so his uncle too. His uncle says to him," By the way, I have some good news for you. The officials have decided to lift the arrest warrant that was issued in your name. So, now that means we all are standing beside you. Dev, go out there and make that Aksh feel what we really are capable of doing. By the way Dev, do you know someone by the name of Gaurav?"

Dev says," I only remember one Gaurav; he used to be Pallav's friend during the school days. But, why are you asking me this?"

His uncle says," Dev, when we removed the mask of the Aksh that you left unconscious on the streets, we found that it was someone named Gaurav. He is in police custody for now and we have also sent his blood for forensic lab to do the testing." After listening to his uncle, Yaksh steps out of his house.

This for the first time Yaksh was supposed to be seen on the streets in the daytime.

Yaksh didn't know where to go to find Aksh but he knew what he has to do in order to force Aksh out. He goes straight to his new house. He blows up the security and makes his way into the house. He beats every single guard on his way. He ferociously searches for Pallav but he could not find him.

The time he was searching for Pallav, landline phone rings up. Yaksh picks up the phone and says," Who is this?"

On the other side was Aksh. He says," Dev, you have reached my home. That's too fast of you. Do you know what; people lose their common sense when they act too fast? You came to my house and didn't even thought that I know who you are and with who all people your heart is attached to. Dev, I have got someone for you." Suddenly, Vidya yells hard on the phone and Dev is fired up now.

Aksh takes the phone back and says," So, how did you like my surprise?"

Yaksh says," You coward!! Using a woman to defeat me. Tell me where are you? I am coming for you. Find a better place to hide."

Aksh says," Dev, first try to exit that place safely. If you are able to do so then meet me in the evening at your old house. I have sent in a few gifts for you. I hope you will love it."

Aksh hangs up the phone. Yaksh puts the phone down when he listen the noise of helicopters hovering over the house. Yaksh could easily see that they were too heavily armed and could easily make out that they too were in no mood to play hide and seek with him. Yaksh realizes there is no use of waiting for them to strike but before Yaksh could even fly out a missile lands into the house and blasts right behind him. He is thrown in one corner of the house. Yaksh loses his cool and decides to make his move.

CHAPTER 39

Yaksh could easily see that the only way out was to take the helicopters down and he was in mood to show any kind of mercy on them. He gathers all his strength, flies high and takes glimpses at the number and positions of the helicopters. The helicopters were four in number and had covered the house from all four sides. Upon seeing their target high in the air, the helicopters open fire at Yaksh. Yaksh decides to counter them one by one and therefore he tears apart one of the helicopter in two pieces that was heavily raining bullets on him after safely landing the pilots and the crew on the ground.

Yaksh throws the two pieces towards the other two helicopters hitting them severely. The hit was so strong that crew could not even react and the two helicopters get blasted away and lands in the surroundings of the house. Yaksh was clearly in no mood to save anyone now. The fourth and the last helicopter stopped firing at him. Maybe, they too sensed that it was of no use. They turn around and try to run away.

Yaksh says to himself," You are too late to do that."

Yaksh catches the helicopter by its tail, swings it hard round and round and then throws it straight into the middle of Pallav's house. The helicopter blasts into flames and so does the house too. The entire house was now left to nothing. There were flames burning all around the place.

Even after taking down all the helicopters, Yaksh was too caught in his act that for a moment he forgot about Vidya. He was now getting fired up and wanted to save her at any cost. But, he was forced to wait as it was late afternoon and he was supposed to meet Aksh and Vidya in the evening.

Since Yaksh had time in the afternoon, he decides to take some rest near his old house where no one could see him. He does this so that he can easily patrol the place and come to know whether Pallav too will be accompanying Aksh and Vidya or not.

Yaksh was waiting for time to go by on one of the terraces of a tall building. The shadows were getting larger when Yaksh hears the noise of high speed cars squealing and sees them stopping by their house. It was a large convoy which Aksh had brought with him. But, surprisingly for few moments no one got down from any of the vehicle. Then, one of the car's doors opens up and Vidya gets down from the car.

Aksh too flies in and lands near Vidya. He forces her into the house. The rest of the convoy simply turns and leaves. Only one of the vehicles of the convoy stays back in which there was only a driver seated and no one else. Yaksh was too surprised to see all this happening.

He was shocked at the brimming confidence of Aksh. Maybe, Aksh was now too over confident that he will going to finish off Yaksh. Whatever it maybe but it was really absurd to see all this. The sun sets in and Yaksh jumps off the building and lands straight in front of his house. He could still feel the pain in his muscles but was continuously trying to hide it.

Yaksh was inching close to an end; who knows whose end it will be? Yaksh steps into the house and sees Vidya sitting on a chair. He also sees Aksh standing right beside her and therefore he stops at a distance from them. Aksh says to Yaksh," I am impressed, Dev."

Seeing Vidya look a little astonished, Aksh says," Oh dear!! Remove your mask, Dev. Let her confirm your real identity. It's really shocking that you never told your lover who you really are? Dev, common on man, you should have at least told her."

Yaksh forcefully removes his mask and says," It doesn't matter now. You have already told her. Aksh let her go. It's between the two of us."

Aksh says," Do you know what Dev, the moment I came to know who you really are; I went through your every single detail of your life."

Yaksh says," So, what?"

Aksh says," Dev, we all have weaknesses and these weaknesses become a source of our death. Did you ever tried to discover that how a bullet pierced your skin when you were seen last and not ever before that? Did you, Dev?"

Yaksh nods in disapproval. Aksh says," I knew it, Dev. Anyone could have easily picked it up and could have destroyed you but it was written in my destiny to finish you off. The fact is that your emotions soften you. You lose control over your powers when you are emotionally challenged. It's the easiest way to kill you. So, I would prefer it rather we fight each other out. I can hurt you more although you are already severely injured. What's the point in that? It will going to end the way I want."

Yaksh was completely silent. Aksh continues," I brought Vidya for a special purpose over here. She needs to do me a favor."

Aksh takes a hand gun out and forward it towards Vidya. He says to her," Vidya, shoot and finish Dev."

Vidya though a little shocked but still confidently says," I will never do it."

Aksh says to her," Don't worry!! Dev will himself going to force you to shoot him."

By saying this, Aksh takes out another gun and points it at Vidya's head. Aksh says," Now Dev, convince her to shoot you or else I will shoot her. You have 5 minutes and your time starts now."

Dev knew exactly what to do. He goes close to Vidya. Vidya was still sitting on the chair. Dev was on his knees in front of Vidya. Vidya was continuously saying," I will not going to do it."

Dev says," Stop it, Vidya. Don't act childish. Just do it what he orders you to do."

Dev was getting frustrated as time was running out. He was trying to stay calm and cool. He says very politely to Vidya," I murdered your father, Vidya. Look at me as your father's murderer and not as you know me. Vidya, just do it. Do it for my sake."

Vidya says," I will go to lose you, Dev."

Dev says," Vidya, listen to me carefully. You will never going to lose me. I promise you this bullet will never going to affect me. Just do it."

Dev was now completely broke. He knew he was flowing in his emotions. But, he needs to save Vidya. Dev says to Vidya," Vidya, trust me. No one can take me away from you. You said it you wanted to punish me. This is the opportunity. Shoot me right across my heart."

Vidya was still unwilling to shoot Dev. Dev says," Vidya, take the gun. Just take it."

The time was running out. Dev shouts at her," Vidya, take it and shoot."

Vidya though unwilling takes the gun from Aksh and aims at Dev. Aksh says," Very good, Dev. Just go on. Common on, Vidya."

The last 30 seconds were left. Dev was still sitting on his knees. Aksh starts the countdown. Dev says to her," Believe me, Vidya. It's all going to be alright. Just do what he demands from you and the rest I will handle it."

Vidya starts to point the gun towards Dev when the last 10 seconds were left. Aksh too points his gun at Vidya's head. Dev for the last time shouts at her," Shoot me, Vidya."

And Vidya shoots; right across the heart of Dev. Dev falls with a wry smile on the ground. He still had some breath left in him but definitely he was about to die. Vidya shouts at Dev," I am sorry, Dev but you deserved it." Aksh says to him," Dev, I forgot one thing. We didn't complete our introduction. I am still left to remove my mask and let you know who I really am. So, stay awake."

Aksh was about to remove his mask when Dev closes his eyes forever.

CHAPTER 40

Dev was dead now. Aksh after removing his mask leaves with Vidya in their car. Dev's body was left in the house unattended.

Mean while Dev after his death goes straight to heaven. He finds himself standing by the huge and magnificent entrance of the heaven. Dev notices that he was dressed just like the native people; in pure white clothes but there was only one thing that was differentiating him from his male counter parts. He was not having a crown like ring on his head like angels do in most of our fairy tales. He was about to step in when a number of native people surrounds him and starts to whisper," See, our Father's son is back."

Dev could not understand not even a single thing what they were saying. Suddenly, a couple of white horse along with a few chariots stops by Dev and one of the men on the horses gets down and kneels before Dev and says," Our respected Father's son, we welcome you to your home. Our Father wants to see you. We are here to escort you to his palace."

A magnificent white horse driven chariot makes way for Dev to step in. Dev walks towards the chariot and sits in the back seat. The driver rides the chariot straight to the palace. On the way, Dev witnesses the magnificent beauty of the heaven. He could now easily understand why this place was termed as "Heaven". The chariot reaches its destination and stops right at the entrance of the palace. Dev steps down from the chariot and walks towards the entrance of the palace.

Dev discovers a court man standing at the entrance waiting for him. Dev walks up to the court man and greets him. The court man says to him," It's so good to see you. It's an honor to have a glimpse of you. I am here to give you a code of conduct inside the palace. See, when you enter the palace, stay quiet. Speak only when you are asked to do so."

Dev says," Why? What's happening inside?"

The court man says," They are going to judge you."

Dev says," But, who and why?"

The court man says," See, though you are a son of our creator but still you were sent in as an experiment. So, there are various wise men along with our creator who are present inside and they will go to judge you."

Dev says," Can't I meet my father all alone?"

The court man says," Once, you pass their judgment."

Dev asks," And what if I fail?"

The court man says," Don't ask me that. You might be having some idea as to what happens to those who fail the wise man's judgment."

Dev nods in disapproval. The court man says," They are vanished forever. Their existence gets over the moment they are declared a failure."

Dev could now easily feel it was like an 'Agni Pariksha' for him in order to be treated as his Father's true son.

The door opens up and Dev along with the court man enters. Dev could easily spot that various wise men were none other than the various gods and goddesses. Dev sees at a far sight, right in the middle, there was a big throne.

A very old man was sitting on the throne. He could easily understand who the old man could be?

As said by the court man, Dev walked and stood right in the middle of the room and stayed quiet for he was supposed to answer only when asked to do so. The proceedings begins when the court man says," Respected wise men, you are now permitted to ask anything from Dev that will help us improve our judgment."

Lord Thunder begins by asking," Dev, how are you?"

Dev says," I am doing well. The feeling of being our creator's son is slowly—slowly soaking in."

Lord Agni rises and asks," It's too generous of you Lord Thunder for asking such questions from him. Coming straight to the point Dev, we all including our creator have gone through your day to day schedule on earth and what astonishes us is that though you were able to take every evil segment of the society down but when it came to your brother, you failed. How?"

Dev says," I tried but I was not able to overcome Aksh."

Lord Agni says," That's whom I am talking about."

Dev was taken aback. He just couldn't get it right. He says," What are you talking about?"

Father steps in and says," Dev, you know it that your brother and Aksh are the same. Don't you?"

Dev was shocked like anything else. There was a sudden turnaround of thoughts in Dev's mind. But, he knew exactly what to do. He says," You must be joking right."

Lord Agni steps in and lands a tight slap on Dev's face and says," Don't you dare talk like that to our creator."

Dev says," See, I have already had too much of a beating. I am not taking any more of this." With this, Dev pushes Lord Agni hard. Father steps in and says," Stop it."

Father continues and orders," Lord Agni, get back."

Dev says to Father," Please, keep it simple."

Father says," Dev, Aksh is no one else but your brother itself. He is thriving on the blood you donated to him seven years ago. Your powers lie in the royal blood you have. You donated your powers along with the blood you donated to your brother to save him. He used it in the wrong direction and stood against you and you were never able to make yourself understand that it was your brother himself."

Dev now got it straight. But, he wanted something else. He stood head down rejected. Father says to him," Dev, I am sorry to say but you have failed, my son. You must have been told what happens to those who fail."

Dev didn't wanted it to end like this. He says," Father, would you grant me my last wish?"

Father says," Make it fast."

Dev says," I want you to hug me like a father-son warmly hugs each other before you terminate me forever."

Father says," Ok, come, have your last wish."

Dev walks towards his Father. Father stands up from his throne and finds Dev standing right in front of him. Dev says to his Father," Father, you rendered no help to me on earth and you think I would have done all by myself. How could you have such a narrow thinking? Let's leave it, it doesn't matter now. Give me a hug and I end this."

Dev moves forward to hug his Father. He hugs Dev and Dev utters something in his Father's ears," Please forgive me for what I am going to do now."

The very next moment Dev pushes his Father back and lands a tight punch on his Father's face. Everyone is stunned as to what Dev had done. Dev hit his Father so hard that the latter fall on the ground. His face was towards the ground and was not visible.

Everyone runs towards Dev to beat him and teach him a lesson. By the time, they could reach where Dev was standing; Father gets up from the ground. Father shouts and orders," Stop it."

Dev says," Now, here is the old man again. Listen to him carefully. Maybe, this time he has something new to say."

Everyone looks at their creator and is stunned to see their creator's face. Dev too turns around to see and he too is shocked. Dev hit his Father on the latter's left cheek. The entire left cheek had disappeared into dust and the bones and the muscles could be easily seen. Everyone was brimming with anger and so the Father too.

Dev could easily sense the upcoming danger. But before anyone could do anything to Dev, Father says," Whoever you are Dev, today you have proved me wrong. You too have been affected by the small and petty thinking of these narrow minded creatures. You loathe your humans too much; therefore you are punished to serve an exile of your entire lifetime on earth between your beloved humans. And, also be prepared because any day I will be coming for you and your human dynasty to hunt you all down. I promise you Dev you will be forced to pay a much higher debt than you can ever imagine. Go and serve your exile."

With this, Dev is thrown back on earth. With a great accelerating speed, he impacts the floor of the house so hard that the entire house collapses on him. Dev regains his senses, wears his mask and flies out of the debris to hunt Aksh down.

CHAPTER 41

Pallav and Vidya were returning back with the entire convoy. Vidya was sitting on the left side and was too upset but was continuously looking outside in search of a hope. Pallav says," There is no use of looking out. No one is coming to save you nor this city."

Vidya says," Can you just shut your mouth?"

Pallav says," Vidya, why are you wasting your . . ."

Pallav didn't complete his sentence when suddenly he sees all his cars flying and landing some in the buildings and some upside down in the streets and some even crashed into the shops too. Before he could even react, he too feels gravity less.

Pallav's car gets a roller coaster ride and lands in the middle of the street. The left side door is thrown open and Yaksh takes Vidya out. Before Vidya could even say anything, Yaksh says to her," Go and find a safe place."

Vidya runs and joins the public that was slowly— slowly gathering in the streets. By the time, Yaksh took Vidya out, Pallav had escaped. Yaksh searches for his brother inside the car when suddenly the car blasts off and Yaksh goes flying by and lands in one of the buildings. Actually, Pallav took his mask, put it on and escaped while Yaksh was getting Vidya out. He hides himself and then when he notices that Yaksh is busy searching for him inside the car, he secretly gives fire to the leaking fuel which blasts the car.

Though Yaksh got a hit but he was no longer any weaker now. Yaksh was still stuck in the building when Aksh flies towards him and says," Why, Dev?"

Yaksh says to him," Because, you need to die."

Aksh says to him," Why don't you admit it that you can't beat me?"

Yaksh says," Who said about me defeating you? You will yourself going to die when you will realize that now I am immortal."

Aksh says," What? That can't be possible."

Yaksh says," Accept it. It will be lot easier for you when I will make you rest on your deathbed."

Aksh was now getting boiled up from inside. He attacks Yaksh with a great momentum trying to jam him into the building but Yaksh steps by and uses the same momentum of Aksh to smash him right across not only that building but also many other buildings too.

Aksh tears apart several buildings and lands in an under construction site. Yaksh too flies at the under construction building and starts searching for Aksh. While Yaksh was searching, Aksh suddenly appears from the back and tries to hit Yaksh with a big iron rod but Yaksh again ducks. Aksh gets unbalanced and Yaksh snatches the iron rod form Aksh's hands and then hits him with the same heavy rod with his full power.

Aksh was biting the dust but still didn't want to accept his defeat. He just couldn't think anything rather just to kill Yaksh. He tries many attempts to land strong hit on Yaksh's body but either Yaksh ducked them or used the momentum of Aksh to counter attack him. Aksh was now severely injured. He was grasping for breath. He could easily see his end nearing. He gets down on his knees while Yaksh was standing a few steps away from him.

Aksh gathers his remaining power this time not to hit Yaksh but to fly away. But, Yaksh was now feeling too powerful. Even before Aksh could fly away high in the air, Yaksh catches his one leg and pulls him down in to the ground. Aksh lands deep into the building foundations and as a result of such a strong impact, the entire building tremors and collapses on him.

Seeing this, Yaksh hurries to find whether Aksh is alive or not. Yaksh wanted his brother to live but in prison. He searches for him and removes piles of rods and broken materials when he sees the hand of Aksh. He flies straight towards him and removes the rest of the material that was lying over Aksh.

Aksh was now very close to his death. Yaksh says to him," Brother, look what have you done to yourself?"

Aksh's costume was torn apart from several places. It was complete in dust. Yaksh removes the mask of Aksh so that he can breathe easily. This time Yaksh is not at all surprised when he sees Pallav's face behind the mask.

Pallav seeing no surprises by Yaksh's body language after removing his mask, asks him," When did you came to know about me behind all this? You died before I could even remove my mask in our old house."

Yaksh says to him," Something that one always yearn to know before dying; is kept hideous from us and we are told only once we die. I too came to know about you after my death."

There was a moment of silence when Yaksh too removes off his mask and says," Aksh, it is not our house. It is my house."

Pallav could easily understand what Dev had said. He says," But why, brother?"

Dev says," You are Aksh for me and no one else. My brother died on the day when you were born or else when I created you."

Pallav says," Don't say like that. I know you still love me. If you didn't love me, you would have killed me moments ago and would have not been talking to me like this."

Dev says," Pallav, I am talking to you so as to make you understand that it all ends here and in this way only. You will have to die because of the choices you have made in your life. I am not going to kill you but will wait here till you take your last breathe."

Pallav knew begging for his life was of no use. He angrily says," Dev, it will never going to end like this rather it was never supposed to end like this. Today, you were so close to death facing me. It's hard to imagine what will happen when a complete army of people like you and me comes to hunt you down?"

Dev was taken aback but he says confidently," You don't have to be worried about that. If I can take you down then I can face anything and anyone that comes my way. And I can promise you that." The two brothers gave a glance towards each other; moments after which Pallav takes his last breathe.

By the time Dev ended Pallav's chapter, all the police, emergency services and the public had gathered around the heavily destructed under construction building. Dev wears his mask and comes out of the building carrying something in his hands.

Yaksh searches for his uncle in the crowd. He flies towards him, takes his uncle to a solitary place, hands over the Aksh's mask to his uncle and says," I told you it will end today."

His uncle says," Dev, I am so proud of you. Well done, Dev."

Dev says," Uncle, I want a favor from you."

His uncle says," You are always welcomed to ask from me anything."

Dev says," Uncle, you have to trust me that Aksh is dead and leave Aksh's body in the debris of that building as I have left it. There is no use of putting in the efforts to extract his body. He is dead and finished."

His uncle says," I have no problem with that. But Dev, who was behind Aksh's mask?"

Dev says," Someone who made a lot of wrong choices in his life."

After taking a brief pause, Dev says," Uncle, it was Pallav."

Dev continues," I don't understand why we fail to get this thing that if we are blessed with certain privileges then we have certain responsibilities too associated with them. My royal blood gives me power and when I donated my blood to Pallav, I also donated my powers too. But, he was too foolish to use them for a greater cause."

His uncle says," Dev, that's what defines us. We as humans are those species who always seek the second opportunity in life. Many discover it but those who don't are the ones who end their lives like Pallav did. He too had the privilege but could never realize its true essence. Dev, it would be the best to leave all this behind."

Dev says," Yeah, I too hope it would better be. By the way uncle, I have become homeless now. Can I stay at your place for some time?"

His uncle says," Don't ever say that word again. You are always welcomed at my place."

Dev was about to leave when his uncle says," Dev, I want to tell you certain things but first you recover from all this and then we will talk."

With this, Yaksh leaves and so too his uncle for the post media detailing of the accident.

CHAPTER 42

Days roll by and life returns back to its normal form. Dev recovers from his injuries and gets back to work. He first decides to reconstruct his old house from the left debris. Dev starts off his work and within a brief period, he was even about to finish the reconstruction work when one day he was about to reach his work place and sees Vidya sitting on the staircase at the entrance of his house from a distance.

Vidya has been eagerly waiting for Dev and she simply gives a smile when she sees him entering the parameters of his under construction house. Dev too smiles back. Vidya stands up and starts walking towards Dev. Since they were a distance apart, so Vidya in a little louder voice says," How are you, Dev?"

Dev too in a loud voice says," I am good. Where have you been?"

Vidya says," I was busy preparing my apology speech."

Dev says," Now, what crime have you done? Your apology speech reminds me that I have to say sorry to you for your father's death."

By now, they both were standing close to each other. So, Dev in a very sincere and a low tone says," Please forgive me, Vidya."

To this, Vidya says," Dev, you don't have to say sorry to me rather I have to."

Dev says," Wait, wait . . . First, tell me why I should not apologize to you for killing your father?"

Vidya says," Because, you never killed my father."

Dev says," Are you out of your senses? I threw your father out of the window from 19th floor of his office?"

Vidya says," Yes, you did but still you didn't kill my father."

Dev says," You must have a better explanation for whatever you are saying."

Vidya says," I have one. When I shot you here some days back, Pallav told me everything."

Dev says," Tell me, Vidya. What did he told you?"

Vidya says," After you died, he said that the night you killed my father you were so brimming with emotions that you were not thinking logically. You were just doing whatever you thought was supposed to be done and when he told you to kill my father he doubted that you might not do it. So, what he did was that he himself went and killed my father before you could even reach that place. He placed my dead father near the window chair and waited in the dark shadows to see what you will going to do. And you did exactly what he thought of. He knew you can't kill my father with your bare hands and so you just simply threw him out from the window. He wanted to blame you for my father's death and this way he got success in his plan. When you returned back to the hospital to see your brother, had you opened his ward's door you would have easily come to know what all had happened because as soon as your blood entered Pallav's body, it healed all his scars and he was much more powerful than ever before. But, my phone rang and you never got the chance to open that door."

Dev says," Oh my God!! Such a big lie. How could he do this to me? I loved him like anything else."

Vidya comes closer to Dev and hugs him to console him.

Dev whispers in Vidya's ears," That means what all I did in the past seven eight years was based on a lie."

Vidya supports Dev and makes him sit on a bench and says," Dev, I want to tell you something and also want to apologize for the same."

Dev was dead silent. Seeking an opportunity to speak, Vidya was about to start when Dev puts his hand on Vidya's lips and says," It's not a good time to give me another shock. Leave something for the future too."

Vidya sensing the emotions and present state of Dev decides to leave her secret to be spilled out in the future. Vidya trying to cheer up Dev; says," But tell me, Dev. How you came back from the dead?"

Vidya could see a smile coming back on Dev's face. Dev stares at Vidya. Vidya says," Why are you smiling? You did a magic trick or what that you survived even your death or are you immortal?"

Dev says," Don't go so far in your thinking. It's simple. I revolted my and this entire universe creator."

Vidya says," You think I am stupid that I will going to believe this."

Dev says," Yes, I did. I slapped our creator right on his face and therefore as a return gift he exiled me forever on earth."

Vidya was stunned and says," Have you gone mad? How could you do this to him?"

Dev says," I thought it to be my best available option and therefore I did it."

Vidya says," And, now what?"

Dev says," He will never going to accept me even though I am his son."

Vidya says," But, after what all you did to Aksh he will definitely going to accept you?"

Dev says," Nope because there is no way by which he can come to know what I am doing on earth."

Vidya says," But why?"

Dev says," That's what the treaty says."

Vidya says," What treaty?"

Dev after giving a little thought says," You can call it Treaty of my Birth."

Vidya says," But why, Dev? Why did you choose us over your father up in the heaven?"

Dev says," I wanted to finish what I had started. And don't be so emotional, they too were interested in terminating me forever. I too wouldn't have survived there too for long."

Vidya says," But still Dev, you should had accepted their decision."

Dev says," That you are saying Vidya. Didn't you want me back when you came to know that Pallav and not I killed your father?"

Vidya says," I wanted but not by paying such a high cost."

Dev says," Vidya, I chose us over them because I too have realized that though we are weak; we commit mistakes but still we can fight back. If humanity needs to be saved then it could be done only by staying amidst you all people and not by giving orders from the top. Vidya, I believe in you and in all these people because we have such a powerful asset of feelings and emotions with us that it can make us stand tall against all the thunders and calamities. I chose human emotions over our creator's decision to terminate me."

Vidya was convinced for now. After a brief gap of silence, Vidya feels to lighten up the mood, so she says," So, what's next?"

Dev says," Haven't thought much; will have to ensure that no evil crops up from anywhere now."

Vidya says," You will remain a Sadu for your entire life. I am asking what have you thought about us?"

Dev says," Who us?"

Vidya says," You leave it, Dev. You always leave the thinking part for me."

Vidya gets up from the bench and comes in front of Dev and gets down on her knees and says," Mr. Dev, if you are free enough from your superhero stuff; I, Vidya Bansal, would like to propose you to marry me."

It was a moment of ultimate delight for Dev but he couldn't express anything. He holds Vidya by her shoulders; lifts her up from the ground and says," Vidya, I would love to."

Vidya says," Thank you, Dev." She turns around and was about to leave when Dev says," Vidya, wait a minute. I have not finished yet." Vidya turns back and Dev continues by saying," Vidya, I love you but this world will not allow us to stay together. Yesterday, Pallav used you against me. Tomorrow there could be someone else who would do the same. Vidya, I am not strong enough to see you in pain because of me. I might not be able to save you all the time even though I can't think of a day when I will be forced to choose between you and the rest of the human race. So Vidya, don't take in other sense but I can't marry you for your own sake."

Vidya steps forward in anger, moves closer to Dev and sensing a burst of anger, Dev takes a step back. Vidya says," Don't worry, I will not going to slap you today rather I feel happy that you are much wiser in your decisions. But still Dev, I will wait for you when such day comes that you yourself will realize that we could be together again."

Hearing this, Dev says," Thank you, Vidya."

Vidya says," Your welcome. But this should not mean that you can fall in love with someone else."

Dev gives a smile to Vidya and with this Vidya turns around and leaves. Dev too gets back to his unfinished work.

Finally, after reconstructing his house from the left debris, Dev tries to convince his uncle to leave the latter's house and move back to his old house by saying," Uncle, that house is a storage of all the memories of the people that always trusted and believed in me. Since, now I have only those memories left with me, so I wish to keep them fresh by staying in my old house. Instead, I suggest you to make a permanent shift with me to my renovated house."

His uncle says," I would love to. But, I can't. I, like you, don't have such fond memories of that house. I prefer to stay here but you better go and relive the fond memories that you have."

Dev replies," Uncle, sometime it's better to move on and leave our past in the past itself. I know it hurts when that house reminds you time and again the loss of your friends or my parents but they are gone now and someday you will have to accept that too."

His uncle says," No, that's not the point. That house reminds me that your parents' life went in vain because they never succeeded in giving a right direction to Pallav's life."

Dev says," No, it didn't. Though Pallav turned out to be a failure but also they were able to produce a gem like me."

His uncle says," Dev, you were tailor made from birth itself to lead a perfect life but Pallav was not."

His uncle takes a deep breath and says," Leave it, Dev. Rather, I will try to take some time out for a visit at your new house."

Dev says," Yeah, I know. You are a very busy man now, Head of Police Department, Mr. Atul Kulkarni. Congratulations for your promotion. By the way, I will come and meet you soon since we have some unfinished business left."

His uncle understood what Dev meant by unfinished business and says," Thanks for your compliments and also I am too looking forward to meet you at the earliest."

At last, Dev leaves and moves back to his re-constructed old house while his uncle stays on in his own house.

CHAPTER 43

After shifting back, Dev as Yaksh used to be occasionally seen taking some night trips across the streets to ensure the safety of the citizens but also he too was now relieved as the crime had almost vanished from the streets since Pallav departed. On one such occasional night trip, he sees his uncle standing in the balcony of the latter's office. Yaksh flies and holds himself in the air at a distance in front of his uncle. His uncle sees him and then carefully checks whether they are alone or not. Once confirming, he signals Yaksh to come in and he himself goes into his office to fetch some files. At the same time, Yaksh lands in the balcony and waits for his uncle to come out. After taking the necessary files, Atul comes out in the balcony when he sees Yaksh keenly observing the silence of the city.

His uncle greets him by saying," It feels so good to see a city breathing so peacefully."

Dev removes his mask and says," Yeah, that's true. So, what have we left now to finish off?"

His uncle says," There have been some strange accidents that came to my notice which occurred on the same night when you killed Pallav."

Dev says," What is so strange about them that it made you so worried?"

His uncle says," Dev, there have been some strong rumors in the air that Sarraf is back in the city and this time he is here with a plan. But, he is completely untraceable. Secondly, a group of specialized highly trained biologists have gone missing. Third, Gaurav escaped the jail parameters but good news is that we were able to test his blood before he escaped. His blood resembled that of your brother's and when I tried to get an exact match of Gaurav's blood, I was surprised to discover but it pointed at your royal blood. Last, there has been a strange robbery at a bank. The strange part is that it was not an ordinary bank but rather a blood bank. And the thing which is more surprising is that the culprits only took a single bottle of stored blood. When I searched it further, I came to know that it was your leftover blood that you donated to your brother which they robbed from the bank."

Dev was dumb struck. He didn't know what to say. Accidentally at the same moment, a thought come across Dev's mind. He says," Now, I understand what Pallav meant on his deathbed."

His uncle says," Dev, I do not want you to get disturb. I just wanted you to be informed about all this. For now, you better take a break because it's peacetime. It's all over. We won, Dev."

Dev says," Uncle, I can easily see what all is heading straight towards us. This silence is not that succeeds a won battle but it's the silence that precedes a thunderous storm."

Dev moves across his uncle, puts on his mask and before leaving says," It's not the end but a beginning."

Before Dev's uncle could turn around, Yaksh had disappeared into thin air.